BRIDGEND LIBRARY AND INFORMATION

3 8030 60065 336 7

Orphans of Chance

By the same author

Stitched
Deceived
Stone Cold

Orphans of Chance

Peter Taylor

ROBERT HALE · LONDON

© Peter Taylor 2012
First published in Great Britain 2012

ISBN 978-0-7090-9904-8

Robert Hale Limited
Clerkenwell House
Clerkenwell Green
London EC1R 0HT

www.halebooks.com

The right of Peter Taylor to be identified as author
of this work has been asserted by him in accordance with the
Copyright, Designs and Patents Act 1988

2 4 6 8 10 9 7 5 3 1

BRIDGEND LIB & INFO SERVICE	
3 8030 60065 336 7	
ASKEWS & HOLT	3597954
	£19.99

Typeset in 11/14.7pt Palatino
Printed in Great Britain by the MPG Books Group,
Bodmin and King's Lynn

*As ever, every word for my father
and my brave, Highland mother*

PROLOGUE

Will Niven sat on the bench at York Station gazing into the eyes of the man next to him. He was not surprised that he still had that slightly glazed look that had come upon him when, about half an hour ago, Will told him why he'd asked for this meeting. This little trip out from Middlesbrough to York had only taken an hour, but in Will's state of health it had felt like a marathon and he was tired now.

He could remember visiting an aunt in York when he was a toddler, his first real holiday, so he supposed there was a certain irony in the fact that this would be the last time he would venture away from home. Today, his business with this man was his final attempt to put his affairs in order, to do the last thing he could for his son. It felt as though his life had come full circle.

'Was it easy to find me?' the man said.

Will shook his head. 'I hired a private detective. Your name isn't too common and he went down some dead ends but I remembered your age. The other candidates were older or younger, so that helped.'

'It's a noble thing you're doing,' the man said.

Will dismissed the remark. He didn't want or need praise. As he'd already explained, he wanted something else and that response was too non-committal for his liking. The man sensed that and had the grace to blush.

'So what do you think of my proposal?' Will said, getting back to business, hoping for a straight answer. 'I can understand if you back off. I'm asking a lot, I know. Tell me no and I'll walk away and you can get on with your life and hear no more about it.'

A disembodied voice announced train times over the tannoy. While they waited for silence to return, the man leaned back, his chin cupped in the palm of his hand in the manner of a thinker in repose. Will thought he looked like a man in a quandary and, if he had to think about it that much, it was no good. He was nearly sure the response would be negative and this was going to be a wasted trip.

'You can't do it, can you?' he said, unable to help himself.

The man shook his head. 'You've mistaken my hesitation. You see, I feel like I've been given a present but won't be able to open it.' Will was glad to hear the genuine emotion in his voice. 'It's a case of look don't touch and that's hard.'

'I understand that, but there'll be a time. I have to trust you to choose it wisely. Anyway, he'll need time after I....'

The man stared at him. 'Don't worry, I get that. I owe you a debt of honour that I can never repay. Even your coming here—'

Will shook his head cut him short. 'You owe me nothing. It was a gift I was given.'

The man nodded sadly. A train hurtled through the station, its passengers a blur of faces staring out, then they were gone never to be seen again, as though they existed in another world, nothing to do with this one and, like tourists, were only looking in for a passing moment.

The man cleared his throat. 'If it's a watching brief, I should know where he works.'

Will Niven smiled to himself. His time and energy hadn't been wasted after all.

'He's a detective sergeant. His DCI is called Snaith – his immediate boss Johnson.'

The man's eyebrows shot up. 'Surely not Tom Johnson?'

'That's him. But how—'

'As you probably have found out, I used to be a bobby

twenty years ago, before I went into the security game. Tom was a good pal back then. We still exchange Christmas cards. I trust him enough to explain the situation to him and I know he won't let it prejudice him.'

'When it's time, only you can decide. It'll be in your hands.'

The man looked at his watch. 'I'll have to go,' he said. 'They'll be expecting me at the office. I said half an hour and it's been over an hour. I thought I was meeting a client, didn't expect—'

Will rose to his feet. 'Sorry for approaching you like this but I thought it best you heard it straight from my mouth, nobody else around, just you and me.'

'Best way,' the man agreed as they shook hands. 'I'll be in touch.'

He reached out, placed a hand on Will's shoulder. 'Thanks doesn't seem enough for what you've done, but – thanks.'

'Your turn now. Good luck.' Will said.

Hiding his tears, he turned away, with a feeling of relief started for the platform where the last train for Middlesbrough would leave soon. Now that he had done as much as he could, he was ready to sever his earthly ties, and surrender to the enemy he couldn't defeat.

CHAPTER 1

Three months later

Detective Sergeant John Niven sat at the bedside, stared down at the ravaged face and wasted body that made a man who had once been strong and bright eyed more like a little boy aged prematurely. Every day for six weeks he'd come to the James Cook hospital whenever he could, watched Will Niven deteriorate, feeling so helpless knowing the end was inevitable.

Why had a good man to suffer like this? Couldn't the reward for a life well lived be a painless passage to the beyond, the hell of an agonized death be reserved for all the scum out there who had no respect for the sanctity of life, their own or that of others. He sighed in frustration. He was so tired and it was a worn out question. It wasn't like that anyway. Every man had his time. It was just a matter of fate how you departed this earth. You might as well howl at the moon, try to change the wind. Acceptance was all.

His father opened his eyes. Even in his pain a spark flared in them as he recognized his adopted son, a spark John knew sprang from the love in his soul, from a kindness that was for everyone. You gave love, you got it back. His heart filled and he cursed his powerlessness to help.

'Where's Gill?' his father asked, reaching out with a bony hand.

'She'll be coming,' John said, taking it.

'Not many like her, John.' The voice was distorted like a wind groaning through trees.

Niven forced a smile, nodded. Gill was his girlfriend of three years. She had been staunch during his father's illness, supporting both of them.

The old man stretched for a glass of water on the cabinet. Niven beat him to it, held it to his lips, let him sip. As he stretched to replace it, his father gripped his hand.

'You know I've always been proud of you,' he rasped. 'Pat – she was too; she died too young, your mother.'

Niven swallowed hard. Pat his adoptive mother had died six years ago and it still hurt sometimes to hear her name on his father's lips. If Pat and this exceptional man hadn't taken him when he was an infant, where would he have ended up? Fate again, but this time working in his interest. For so many others the dice fell the wrong way, didn't it?

'Never thanked her properly,' he said. 'Both of you,' he added, correcting himself. 'Should have done – long ago.'

The old man's expression darkened. 'It never made you unhappy, did it, John? Hate to think—'

'No! 'John said, cutting him off. 'Don't think that. I was never unhappy with you.'

The aged eyes blinked, then focused on him, searching through weariness and pain.

'You wondered though. Didn't you?'

Even now, John found it hard to lie under his step-father's scrutiny. Those wise eyes had always seemed to see right through him and how could you lie to somebody you loved?

'Speculated sometimes. When you told me I was adopted it was strange for a while, then I forgot about it. Anyway, I wouldn't have changed anything, even if I could have.'

His old man lay back on the pillow and breathed hard. 'When you were very small,' he said, 'I used to worry about your temper, but you got on top of it.'

'I remember. Like a volcano, sometimes. Couldn't have a temper like that now, not in my job. Wouldn't last.'

'You never – asked many questions.'

Niven knew what he was referring to and nodded. He wished his father would leave the subject of his adoption alone. They'd rarely discussed it in the past. But his father's mind had the habit of going back, now that he hadn't long left to live. This outburst was just part of that.

The ill man suddenly raised his head, staring at him. 'Don't bother looking, now,' he said, gripping Niven's wrist. 'Let sleeping dogs lie – best thing!'

There was no need to explain. Niven understood what he meant. Why was he so concerned?

'Don't worry,' he answered. 'I've come this far without the need. Just you take it easy, Dad. Don't worry about anything.'

The old man sighed. 'Glad you feel that way. Best....' But he was too weary to finish the sentence and, closing his eyes, drifted off to sleep.

An hour later Niven walked out of the hospital, paused at the door. In the distance, he could see the lights of the traffic scurrying in fits and starts along the congested Marton Road; he envied the people in the cars returning from a hard day's work to the sanctuary of their homes, the bosoms of their families. Further off, on the broad horizon, the last red streaks of a dying sun lingered like wounds. Another day had gone never to be reclaimed and this was one he would never forget. A good man, the best, had just passed away and was travelling now, he hoped against hope, to a better place.

He felt a sudden sense of abandonment which he knew was selfish. Part of him wanted to follow, go with the old man to whatever lay beyond that dying sun because he knew part of him had already gone with him anyway. But even as he thought it he dismissed the notion as unworthy. His father would have wanted him to live his life, make the best he could of it, endure. Anything less would have been a waste of the care he'd received from him and Pat.

As he sucked in lungfuls of air, people passed by him in droves but, isolated in so many memories, he was only dimly aware of them until someone calling out his name broke into his reveries. He looked to his left and saw Gill standing there gazing at him.

'Are you OK,' she said, when she had his attention. 'I worked late, thought I'd miss you. How is he? I....'

When she saw he was only half aware, her voice ground to a halt, hit the buffers. He didn't need to speak; his glassy eyes spoke for him, telling her everything.

'Was he in much pain?' she asked, tears forming in her own eyes as she brushed her long red hair back and put her arms around him.

He shook his head. 'Went in his sleep, thank God.'

Linking arms, they walked to the car in silence. Having her beside him made a difference and took the edge off his feeling of abandonment.

As they drove onto Marton Road, Gill spoke.

'I'll stay at your place tonight, if you want.'

He nodded. 'It would help.'

CHAPTER 2

Niven sat back in his seat as DC Jim Short accelerated away. They'd been tying up loose ends from a previous case and their shift was nearly finished. The funeral was a week past, thank God. People had been kind and he'd appreciated it but, however well meaning, all those words wouldn't bring his father back. He'd been glad to return to work, to routine, even the mind numbing variety like today. It seemed to be the best anti-dote to his grief.

They were on Linthorpe Road in the centre of Middlesbrough and it was that time of day when people were either drifting home ready for their beds or heading off to the night clubs. Short pulled in to the kerb next to a fish and chip shop.

'You fancy some to take home?' he said, sniffing the air like it was perfume and sighing as the smell from the shop drifted in.

Niven yawned. 'After that performance, how could I resist.'

Short was straight out of the car. 'Bit of a queue, John. Don't fall asleep, will you?'

'Don't be embarrassed to ask for scraps with mine,' Niven called after him with a sly grin. 'Always feel sorry for the leftovers in life. My compassionate side coming out.'

Short raised a mocking eyebrow then headed for the shop. As he settled down to wait, Niven watched people drifting through the night, mainly the groups of lads larking about with exaggerated *bonhomie*. Nobody in those groups wished to let the side down, nor give even a hint that he wasn't up for it, whatever 'it' was. It was harmless most of the time. But experience told him there was always one who, under the influence of old uncle alcohol, would raise the stakes too high in order to impress, and it only took that one to lead the others to cause mayhem.

He reprimanded himself for his cynicism. He'd been a little daft on occasion himself and since had always told himself he wouldn't be ruled by cynicism like some coppers he knew. Trouble was, over the last few months he'd felt a change in his thinking. More and more he believed he and his colleagues were only blowing the chaff away, not chopping at the rotten roots of crime, not making a big enough difference. Time consuming paperwork, an obsession with human rights to the point of parody, lenient sentencing, soft prisons, were all making him question his chosen profession and wonder whether he should get out before he was trapped too deep in a rut.

The car door opened, interrupting his thoughts. Short leapt inside, hurled his fish and chips into the passenger foot well, pointed to a figure in a grey hooded top further along the pavement.

'What?' Niven said.

The younger man's face was flushed with excitement. 'That's Jack Cannon. I'm nearly sure.'

Niven straightened. Cannon was a gangster who'd been on the run for a year. The received wisdom was that he'd swapped sunny Middlesbrough for somewhere in the Med. He glanced at his watch. Ten minutes to the end of their shift. But that didn't matter. If Shorty's enthusiasm hadn't given him myopia, he'd spotted a big fish, one tasty enough for them and their colleagues to feed off for months. He climbed out of the car, Short following his lead.

'Only one way to find out,' he called over the bonnet of the car. 'But go canny. He's a nasty piece of work.'

They walked fast, side by side, gradually gaining on the

hooded figure who, in the orange glow of the streetlamps, seemed to take on a spectral appearance. Suddenly, he turned off into a side street. Increasing their stride they hurried after him, reducing the distance to twenty five yards; they were tempted to run but didn't wish to risk spooking him. Then, something, a sixth sense or a well honed instinct, made the figure turn his head. Two grim faced men in smart suits bearing down on him was enough of a clue and he burst into a run.

'Damn it to hell!' Niven shouted as they started to run after him. 'Even if its not him, this one's guilty of something.'

He led them through a maze of terraced streets. As they fell further behind, Niven could hear his colleague's laboured breathing and knew his own wasn't great either in spite of the fact both were pretty fit. Finally, their man darted back onto Linthorpe Road and they emerged from the maze of back streets in time to see him sprint past three uniformed specials who watched open-mouthed, heads swivelling between the suits and the fugitive like punters at a tennis match.

'In pursuit!' Niven yelled at them, flashing his warrant card.

They caught on, stepping out of his way. Niven ran on, skidded to a halt, Short bumping into him. They couldn't see Cannon! In desperation, they scanned shop doorways, stepped around a group of lads in tee-shirts and Boro tops who stared at them attired in their suits as though they were aliens. Niven thought that was it; their man had outrun them, disappeared and they wouldn't see him again. Had he managed to cross the road, gone down a street on the other side?

His eyes leapt ahead, ate up the street and narrowed as they zeroed in on a figure twisting its way like a wisp of smoke through a crowd of lads crossing the road. The body language wasn't right – the figure looked like someone wanting to run, but holding back. Niven could see no hood, but the top was grey. He pulled on Short's arm, pointing.

They took off again watching the grey streak until it disappeared into a side street on the other side of the road. A car horn blasted them as they cut in front of it to cross over. Short burst into the street first, then came to a halt as Niven caught him up. Hands on their knees, they gasped for air while a deserted street mocked their efforts.

Cursing his luck, Niven shook his head. 'Suppose those chips will be cold by now.'

But his colleague straightened, stood erect, like a soldier on parade. Something had his attention and it wasn't the thought of those chips.

'Second house from the far end, on the left,' he rattled off, eyes transfixed. 'Think I caught a movement there.'

Niven sighed. 'OK, Hawkeye. Let's hope this is worth the bother, eh!'

CHAPTER 3

They started down the street, walking fast but at a pace that allowed their lungs to recover. Niven knew that if they did trap their man and it was Cannon, a violent confrontation could ensue because he had a history of those, they'd better be ready.

In the glow of the street lights they could see the houses were old but neat and freshly painted. People had made an effort. The one Short spotted was an exception, like a tramp in rags surrounded by toffs in tops and tails. Flakes of paint peeled off the door and window frames, as though the place had a nasty skin disease. The window panes themselves were grimy, opaque with ancient dirt. Where they were visible, rags of curtains had creases like tram lines gone crazy.

Short hesitated, looked to Niven for reassurance. 'Do we go in?'

'You bet,' Niven told him. 'We're in pursuit of a criminal, aren't we?'

Short pulled on the door handle. Surprisingly the door swung open. Niven drew a deep breath, stepped inside, groped for the light switch and pushed it down.

Nothing happened. The interior was dark and gloomy but as his eyes adjusted, Niven made out a stairway to the right. His nose twitched as a rotten smell infiltrated his nostrils. A warning tingle ascended his spine. He didn't like this at all, going into a house virtually blind was the stuff of nightmares. He wondered whether he should call for back-up but knew it would take time to arrive, enough time for the fugitive to slip away. That apart, if this turned out to be just an empty house, the boys in blue would never let them forget it.

'You go upstairs,' he told Short. 'I'll look down here. But go carefully. If you come across our man, call out.'

While Short ascended, he started down the hall on his toes. There was a door on his left which he figured must lead into the living-room. He pushed it open and entered; he found himself in a void of darkness, felt for the light switch, found it, pressed.

Nothing happened! Drawn curtains shut out the street light so that, even as his eyes adjusted, all he could perceive were shapes, hulks of furniture like sombre night creatures on silent vigil. His foot went down on a hard surface – there was no carpet. Heart thudding, he launched himself across the dark room, grabbed the curtains, tore them open, pirouetted as light from a street lamp bled into the room.

He didn't have time to draw breath as a shape launched itself from the couch like an animal roused from its night nest. He watched a hand rise, had barely time to notice it held something long and thin in its grip before it started to descend. At the last moment he moved his head and, as the hand passed inches from his right cheek, his brain registered it was a syringe. Terrified, he watched the needle embed itself in the wooden window-frame, the hand released its grip.

Blood roared in his head. The warning tom-toms in his heart reached crescendo. and every nerve in his body screamed in outrage. He saw a face no more than a foot from his, emaciated, swamped by long matted hair and a beard, it hardly seemed human. Soulless, black eyes leapt out at him and his brain screamed the word, junkie.

The torrent of rage swept him up. He lowered his head, drove it hard at that face, heard the crack as the nose fractured, the animal ululations as the junkie staggered, then a dull thud as he collapsed onto the floor whimpering like a puppy. In the same moment, he felt a blinding pain in his own head. As his legs started to give way he felt for the couch, managed to topple onto it as a black tornado engulfed him.

He was lost, walking alone in a surreal landscape where there was nothing but sand and sea, except for a solitary bundle that lay ahead of him like a isolated island in an endless desert of blinding white sand. As Niven got closer he realized the bundle was a baby sitting straight-backed. He couldn't see its face as it gazed intently at the ocean where waves rose and crashed. How could anyone human leave a baby alone in this infinity of sea and sand he wondered?

He followed the baby's gaze, could see nothing in the water until suddenly two figures rose out of the waves, a man and woman both fully clothed. Niven wanted to cry with relief. The baby was not alone after all. Relief was superseded by terror when the figures started for the shore and he saw that, though perfect in every other way, neither the man nor the woman possessed a face. Where there should have been eyes, a nose, a mouth, there was nothing except a blank parchment of skin. Everything that gave a human an identity was missing. A shiver ran up his spine. Where was he? How had he come to be here?

He dragged his eyes back to the baby who was holding two chubby arms out towards the two figures as though, despite those featureless faces, it recognized them. Just for a second Niven felt a strange sense of empathy with the infant. Then, a great roar issued from the sea and he turned in alarm to see a huge wave rise to dwarf the others and shape itself into a giant mouth. Before he could shout a warning, it rushed towards the man and woman, snapped its jaws down, swallowed them up as easily as a whale feeding on minnows.

Terrified, Niven wanted to pick the baby up and run, but his limbs wouldn't respond and he stood transfixed as the giant mouth opened again and swept towards the shore. He knew it was coming for the baby and him but before he could move it was upon them, jaws snapping down. At the last second, before it engulfed them, the baby turned its face towards him and he saw his own face staring back at him.

CHAPTER 4

Niven woke dripping with sweat, a salty taste on his lips. For a moment, still half in his dream and disorientated, he wondered where he was. Then he felt the ache in his head, remembered the fight and realized he must have blacked out. As his eyes focused in the gloom he saw the junkie stretched out on the floor, recalled the needle missing him by a fraction. A wave of nausea overwhelmed him and he spewed up all over his attacker. Even as he vomited, he felt cold at the thought of the creature passing on aids in that needle. But he didn't have time to dwell on his fate long because he heard the sounds of a scuffle in the hallway. Short had gone upstairs after Cannon; he must need his help.

Moving like an automaton, he stepped around the prone figure at his feet and headed into the hallway where the poor light was just sufficient to make out two figures near the front door locked in a struggle. He saw an arm rising into the air and glimpsing a knife, he realized any second it would plunge down into Short's chest.

Time seemed to stop as Niven experienced an awful prescience. Then it shivered forward again and he grabbed the arm before it could begin its downward arc, drove his knee hard into the man's spinal column. The shock made the attacker drop the knife. He fell off Short, scrabbled towards the door on all fours like a monstrous spider dashing for cover.

Niven ignored him, focused on Short, who tried to rise but fell back. His eyes looked past Niven, stared at his adversary.

'I'm OK, just bruised,' he bellowed. 'Get after him!'

Niven's adrenalin was in full spate. Everything seemed unreal, everything civilized, a mere memory. He honed in on the fugitive who was holding onto the door frame and, letting out a primal roar, launched himself with a force that carried both of them over the threshold and out onto the street. In a tangle of arms and legs, they rolled around on the cobblestones, hitting out blindly. His opponent tried to drag himself away but Niven, releasing a string of obscenities, hauled him back, pinned his arms to the ground with his knees. Now, for the first time, he got a good look at the face. It was the notorious Jack Cannon all right.

The criminal ceased his struggling. He was breathing hard and seemed to realize that he was up against a force he couldn't escape, that there was an irresistible fury, greater than his own, powering the copper whose glassy eyes appeared to have lost all consciousness of time or place.

'OK! Enough!' he yelled. 'You win – this time!'

Fist raised in the air, Niven froze. He heard the voice, understood the words but didn't want to hear them, didn't want to extinguish the fuse inside him when it was so near the dynamite. Why should this low-life have the satisfaction of surrender after what he'd been through in that dark room, the threat of that knife a moment ago? He wanted to pound the miscreant's head, make him understand by sheer force what it was like to be on the receiving end, purge him of his evil. He couldn't hold back and his fist started on its downward path.

Before Niven's fist reached its target a hand grabbed Niven's wrist. Simultaneously, an arm encircled his chest, held him back robbing him of his satisfaction. A voice hissed in his ear.

'Leave it! Can't you see he's done!'

He resisted until, half turning, he registered that whoever was restraining him was in uniform. Gradually, he came back to himself and noticed two other uniforms hovering. As the fog in his mind cleared, he realized the uniforms were the specials they'd encountered earlier and, shrugging the man off, rose to his feet.

The voice came again, grating with him because it sounded so superior, so condescending.

'Calm yourself. Remember what you are.'

Angered by the effrontery of a part-timer reprimanding him after what he had just been through, he turned, ready to unleash venom. Why had he and his mates been so slow on the scene anyway?

But as he looked into the special's knowing blue eyes, he realized that, however hard it was to take, he'd done him a favour. Now most of his anger was directed at himself because he'd come so close to the edge a moment ago he could easily have killed Cannon.

'See to my colleague inside,' he muttered. 'Be careful. There's another feller needs arresting laid out in the living-room. Wait for back-up. He's a mad man.'

Cannon was on his feet, two specials holding onto his arms. They looked like shy apprentices called to a job for the first time, not sure of procedures, so Niven was grateful the prisoner was too exhausted to put up much more resistance. He glanced at the doorway just as Short came through with the blue-eyed special. The DC was holding a shoulder and one of his cheekbones was swollen.

'OK?' Niven enquired.

'Still make my date tomorrow night,' Short said, glaring at the prisoner. He cocked an eyebrow. 'Can I have the pleasure or have you already?'

'Be my guest.'

The DC walked up to the criminal, looked him in the eye. 'Jack Cannon, I am arresting you ...'

He gave him the spiel verbatim, contempt riding on every word. Cannon met his gaze, a half smile on his lips, letting them all know he was down but not beaten, that this was nothing new to him, an occupational hazard.

One of the specials had shown initiative. The words were hardly out of Short's mouth when a police car and van, blue lights flashing, sirens blaring, turned into the street. People who had heard the scuffling were already on their doorsteps. Now more doors opened, more necks did swan impressions. This would be worth a bit of gossip with the neighbours – might even get them on the telly.

Niven gave instructions, the uniforms went into action. Three of them dragged the bearded junkie out of the house. He looked docile enough now, more like a left-over, old time hippy in a happy trance. When both prisoners were cuffed, they were bundled into the meat wagon. One of the constables noticed Short's injuries, his face twist in pain when he moved his shoulder.

'Get you an ambulance, shall I, sir?'

Short shook his head. 'No thanks. I'll be all right.'

'Best you go to hospital and get checked out,' Niven told him. 'Give me the keys and I'll drive the car back to the station.'

Short protested, but Niven insisted and the uniformed constable rang for an ambulance which appeared just as the police vehicles exited the street. Once Short was on his way, Niven turned to the specials who were standing in a huddle on the pavement.

'Thanks lads,' he said, including his helper in the handshakes. 'He was a wrong 'un we'd been after for a long time.'

As they shook, his special helper scrutinized him. From under the peak of his cap those knowing blue eyes somehow conveyed a sense of superiority, seemed to judge him. Niven felt uncomfortable, knew that was down to his own guilty feeling making him hyper-sensitive.

Retracing his route back to the car, he felt weary, his muscles aching from the two violent confrontations. He remembered blacking out, a strange dream, knew that like Short, he should have gone to hospital himself. But it was his total loss of control tonight that was troubling him, more now that he was alone with time to think. He felt he'd just visited part of himself he hadn't known existed, a dark, wild place fit only for demons. He'd been in hairy situations before, but always remained in control. Tonight had been different. He tried to find excuses, telling himself that surely anybody would have reacted like that, that it had been a case of do or die.

He sat a while in the car. The stench of cold fish and chips in his nose was strangely comforting with its connotations of a return to normality. When he started to shake, he knew it was delayed shock and, though it soon subsided, it left a terrible sense of despair in its wake. He sensed it was the cumulative effect of tonight's events and that feeling of not belonging anywhere, of rootlessness, that had been working on him since the funeral. He'd thought he'd known who he was but now he wondered whether another person lurked inside him – a person he didn't know at all and was not so far removed from the scum he dealt with.

CHAPTER 5

'Call me old-fashioned but I want marriage and children one day.'

Niven stared at Gill trying to hold her gaze. He was wondering how this subject had arisen. She was a beautiful, warm woman: his girlfriend. He'd been drawn to her from the first moment he'd lain eyes on her so why, whenever this subject came up, did he feel a gulf opening between them, an ice field he wished he could cross but just couldn't. The fact that she'd had to say those words to him, this proud, caring girl, was bad enough. It should have been down to him. Did he have ice instead of blood in his veins?

He fell silent. It had been only two days since the Cannon arrest. He hadn't told her about it, nor the feelings he'd experienced in the aftermath. How could he articulate to her what he was feeling when he couldn't himself understand it himself?

Gill studied his face, saw his struggle and misinterpreted it. 'Sorry!' she said. 'Not long since the funeral. Insensitive of me.'

That made him feel worse. He thought his father's death should have meant he was ready for marriage and children, a natural progression in a way. But it hadn't. After the other night, his close call, he felt he didn't want to bring a child into a world were you were subject to the whimsical hand of fate. But it was more than that. It was this sense of isolation he felt, not knowing whose blood had formed him. Perhaps deep down this had always been there and it had taken his father's death to bring it to the surface. His rage had led to questions about the void regarding his parents, where much of what he was had probably already been determined. He forced himself to answer.

'Gill, I can't … contemplate having children.' His voice seemed to belong to someone else, distanced, like a far-off echo in a deserted house. 'And marriage is to do with children, isn't it?'

Her face was a mask as she stared at him. He wondered how he could have said it so bluntly. Yet, at that moment, it was how he felt and Gill deserved the truth. He couldn't lie to her, ever.

'You sound so – adamant,' she said arching her back, 'so certain. In the past we talked about one day … as a possibility.'

Niven sighed. 'I'm sorry,' he said. 'Nothing ever stays the same. Viewpoints change.'

Gill's eyes flared at him. 'That means you've changed your feelings for me!'

He shook his head. 'I feel the same about you.'

The silence returned. This time it was a moody, seminal one, as though they were standing on the edge of an abyss, neither able to look into it, fearing what they might see there.

'I think I at least deserve an explanation.'

The coolness in her voice hurt him, but he felt it was well earned.

'Yes,' he said. 'You do.'

He told her about the incident with the junkie and Cannon, how he'd felt, left nothing out.

'Something changed for me,' he concluded. 'I feel like a stranger to myself. Who am I, really? Whose genes do I carry? For all I know my birth parents could have been serial killers. Knowing what's out there, seeing it every day, I don't think it's a fit world for a child.'

She didn't answer, just looked at him, so he rose and went to the bureau, opened it and pulled out a piece of paper. It was his birth certificate which showed his birth mother's name and address, the name she had given him. He placed it on her lap. She opened it and read in silence.

'When did you get this,' she asked, when she was finished.

'I sent for it when I was eighteen, the legal age for such things. Never followed it up though. Felt bad doing it behind Dad's back – still do. Thought it best just to ignore it.'

Gill thrust the certificate back into his hands. 'My father left when I was three years old, never contacted us again. None of this should make a difference. Follow it up if you have to but you know me and I know you. If that's not enough—'

Her reaction surprised him. She'd always understood him, hadn't she? Though he felt he had no right to, he felt angry. He stared back at her, wondering what to say.

Outside, somewhere in the night a motorcycle backfired, the noise like a gunshot intruding into the impasse between them. Niven got up, walked to the window and stood with his back to it: he studied the woman he loved, the slight downturn of the mouth, the sadness in her eyes which he had caused. He knew what he had to do for her sake. Maybe there was a chance he could sort himself out, that these feelings would pass. But what if he didn't? Where would that leave her?

'You deserve better – the best,' he said, clearing his throat. 'Don't take this the wrong way but I think we should try parting for a while. Maybe a bit of time apart will—'

The speed of her reaction surprised him. In an instant she was on her feet, grabbing her coat and handbag. She fumbled in her handbag for her key, threw it on the table.

'OK by me,' she said, eyes firing bullets at him.

Before he could say anything, she tilted her head, threw the door open. He thought she was going to leave without another word, but she spun around in the doorway.

'Maybe you should try to find your birth parents,' she said. 'But I can't see what good it would do.'

He shook his head. 'Sleeping dogs have to lie.'

Before he could say another word, she was gone. The noise of the door shutting behind her was like a coffin lid slamming down on something precious.

CHAPTER 6

John Terrence Brannigan sat on his bed staring at the walls of his cell. He'd heard from his son that Jack Cannon had been arrested days ago; he hadn't been surprised at the news; Jack was a risk-taker with a mad streak. Right now though, he had other things on his mind besides his cousin's incarceration – he started picking at the pockets of his memory, trying to figure whether somewhere along the line he'd sent out signals that he could be played without severe consequences to those who fancied their chances. He didn't think so. Given his gnarled appearance and a physique that was still imposing for a fifty year old, he knew not many would challenge him directly.

But this wasn't like that, this was behind his back and, according to the long-standing mole he had cultivated down at police H.Q., it was two of his oldest compatriots in crime, men who should have known better, who were at it.

Thinking about them, his inner fuse ignited. He leapt from the bed gripped the bars on the window, stared out at the industrial landscape of Teesside, at his town, Middlesbrough, once an infant Hercules, now, like himself, not so sure of its future. On the horizon he could see the hills, parts of the town cosying up to them as though the buildings wanted to crawl away over the top to the Yorkshire Moors, escape to the vastness of the moorland itself. Only months of a two year stretch left, the home straight looming for him now. Easy peasy! He'd done longer sentences with his eyes shut and that was before they'd provided you with Sky television to numb your brain.

He gripped the bars until his knuckles turned white. No doubt about it, his anticipated freedom was under threat. The thought of doing more time was like a knife twisting in his gut. He was too old, his time too precious, to give any more of his life to Her Majesty.

His rage washed through him like a tide of water coming to the boil. The faces of Don Paxton and Jimmy Peacock rose with the tide, shimmered in his brain. He wished they were right there in front of him in the flesh so that he could gut them, feed them to the gulls who swept past his window screeching like banshees.

Forcing the rage down, his mind ran over what he knew. Paxton had been arrested for drug dealing and, according to his source, was fingering him for a post office job he'd done long enough ago to be ancient history. Right now, Paxton was a stone's throw away in the vulnerable prisoners' wing, a sure indication that he'd snitched – otherwise why would he need protection.

Peacock was on the out, but had turned police informer. That was worrying because they went way back, the same as him and Paxton. Jimmy knew things about him, risky things. He'd thought they were old-school, those two and would never give the pigs the time of day. He'd thought they understood it was always us and them, from the minute you were born.

What had changed them? The younger generation coming through? Or had it always been in their characters? Perhaps his absence on the streets hadn't made their hearts grow fonder and they'd become too sure of themselves.

His rage gradually subsided. He'd learned over years that his anger could waste energy better employed elsewhere. This problem required thought ... planning. Those two traitors needed terrifying, made to understand there would be no escaping his wrath if they continued on their present courses: nowhere they could hide. He lay down on his bed again to think it out, came to the conclusion that warning off Peacock wouldn't be a problem but Paxton, sequestered with the vulnerable prisoners for protection, was another matter.

All that day, he brooded on the problem, even missed association. Then, as the sun set and the shadows of the bars lengthened on the wall opposite, he decided. Sliding his left trainer from under the bed, he peeled away the sole, extracted the mobile phone hidden there and dialled his son's number. Darren was like his right arm; he knew that family came before anything and was all that counted. You took care of your own and everybody else could go to the devil in a dog-eat-dog world. He was taking care of his business for him now and he could take care of this for him, too.

His son picked up on the third ring. Brannigan didn't waste time, told him the problem.

'So Paxton's stitching me and Peacock's become dangerous,' he concluded, 'and you're the man who can do something about it, Darren, son.'

'Whatever you want, consider it done.'

Brannigan liked that, liked that his son hadn't hesitated.

'Listen kidda, Paxton's got a younger brother, a small time dealer. He dotes on the scruffy bastard.'

'Billy? Billy the Whizz?'

'You got it. Pay him a visit, son. Give him a right going over. Video it and send it to my phone.'

'Sorted,' Darren said. 'But how will Paxton get to see the show?'

'I have a mucker on his block who has a phone. He'll show Paxton your movie debut. So make it good, eh!'

His son laughed. 'Darren the director. I like that. But what about Peacock?'

'Take some boys round. Give him a going over. Make sure he knows if things go wrong for me, he'll be the one who'll pay the price.'

'No problem. I'll let you know when it's done. The Peacock won't be so proud when we've plucked a few tail feathers.'

They ended the call there. Brannigan felt a warm glow as he prepared for bed. It was reassuring to know he'd brought his son up right, to know what was what, where lines were drawn and woe betide anyone who crossed them. Family was a blessing, wasn't it? Nobody would do for you like the blood of your blood.

CHAPTER 7

Alan Thompson tugged at his collar where the sweat was running down his neck. That sweat wasn't just from the heat: the class in front of him – their desks strewn with cans and crisp packets so that the room looked more like a Macdonald's than a place of learning, were known as the Wild Bunch. Today they'd lived up to their name. His efforts at control had exhausted him. He had nothing left to give. Thank God lunchtime was only a few minutes away.

'You should tell them, sir,' a pasty-faced girl at the front whined, referring to two lads exchanging full on verbals across the classroom. The reprimand from a youngster of fourteen cut through him like a sword. He'd worked hard for his degree in religious studies and then to qualify as a teacher. His failure, the shattering of his ideals, was devastating. There was no doubt about it, he'd been right to resign before his morale collapsed entirely and the little savages picked over his bones. But what else could he do now? Jobs weren't easy to find.

'You can't touch them, can you, sir,' a lad shouted when he heard the girl. 'Only pervs touch kids. Not a perv are you, sir?'

'Shut it!' he said, flushing, longing for the bell, tempted to let them go early.

When the bell went, tasting freedom in the air, the kids charged for the door like a rebel army. A wave of relief swept through him. The prospect of a whole dinner-hour to recharge his batteries, before the next battle clarion, was an oasis in the desiccated waste of his life.

The staffroom was two floors up. As he looked down at the kids in the play areas, he felt like a guard in a prison watchtower, only his rifle missing. How he envied them their energy, those kids! How he hated their indiscipline, the wasted potential he'd thought he could nourish by leading them into the world of ideas and philosophy that separated man from the unthinking beast in the field. It had been three of those beasts, John Terrence Brannigan, Don Paxton and Jimmy Peacock who had damaged his father. But that was another story.

George Preston, a middle-aged teacher, who'd somehow lasted fifteen years here, came to stand beside him.

'Never mind, sunshine,' he said, seeming to guess his state of mind. 'Only weeks to go for you. You're not the first you know. Little blighters have seen a few off in my time.'

Thompson glanced at him, hating the implied superiority. Preston had mastered the art of just saying and doing enough to get by. He envied him his ability to control his classes, but not the fear he inspired with his sarcastic tongue. Perhaps that was the secret, a venomous tongue.

Before he could form a suitable reply, he spotted a crowd gathering in the corner of the play area. Two big lads had hold of a small one and one of the gang, Billy Tyrell – son of a third generation criminal – was standing right over the little lad, his fist drawn back.

Preston saw too. 'Tyrell likes to extort. Passed down father to son, eh! You've a future street thug there. It'll soon be old ladies' handbags. After that? Who knows?'

'We should do something about him,' Thompson said, but even as he said it his voice sounded weak to him, words for words' sake.

Preston cocked an eyebrow at him. 'Prevention not cure. Remember the headmaster's dictum. That means you can't change anything, so look away when you can.'

For him, Preston's stark summation seemed to embody everything that was wrong here, why he and others like him couldn't do the job. The system was bending to breaking point, letting the pupils off with murder. He looked at Preston, saw something in his eyes he thought was mockery, even contempt, reserved for young whippersnappers like him who thought they could change the world. Well, just this once he'd show the old fossil. What had he to lose? He'd be gone in four weeks anyway, wouldn't he?

'I'm going down there,' he said, starting for the door.

'Careful, now.' He heard the chuckle in Preston's voice. 'Prevention not cure, remember!'

'Exactly!' he called over his shoulder. 'I'm going to prevent Tyrell terrorizing that lad.'

CHAPTER 8

Niven and Short were the flavour of the week, with the brass in particular. There was talk of their being put forward for bravery awards. Their chase through the streets of Middlesbrough was referred to as *The Cannonball Run* by some of the wags, alluding to the film of that name. Niven was tiring of being called Bertie, after Burt Reynolds who starred in it. The way he was feeling, he just wished it would all die a death. How could he tell people he was having second thoughts about his career, and other things, with all that good will floating around in the ether?

When his boss DI Johnson rang and asked him to go up to his office, he groaned inwardly because the garbled explanation was that it was something to do with the Cannon case. He hoped it wasn't going to be about the rumoured award. All he wanted to do was move on, forget that night. A whole week and it still hadn't died.

When he entered his office, Johnson was leaning back in his chair, fingers interlinking around his ample stomach. Just for a second, he seemed oblivious to Niven's presence, as though he was in a faraway place, contemplating serious matters. He came around quickly enough, but his face maintained a certain gravity as he gestured for his DS to take a seat. Niven knew him well enough to know he wasn't his usual jovial self and was immediately on guard. Somehow this had the smell of a reprimand.

'You feeling OK these days, John?' he opened, just a semblance of a smile creasing his jowl. He coughed, cleared his throat and Niven thought he caught a whiff of embarrassment.

'Yes, sir!' Niven answered, antenna extending.

'I don't wish to intrude on a private matter, John, but your father's death must have been difficult for you. I remember when my father died. Knocked me for six. Took a while to get it together.'

Niven was perplexed. Johnson was clearly starting down a path, but he had no idea where it was leading, except he had the feeling the subject in question was one neither of them wanted to explore.

'I'm coping, sir.'

'Good! Good!' Johnson said. 'Gill must be a great help. We all need somebody at such times, don't we?'

Niven began to wonder whether the bush telegraph had been at work and he'd heard he and Gill had separated. Gill wasn't the type to blab to everybody about it, but these things had a way of travelling.

Johnson pulled at the loose flesh under his chin. 'You think you could do with some time off? Shoot the breeze as the Americans say. Sometimes people make mistakes if they're put under too much stress.'

'Mistakes,' Niven's brow puckered as he fired the word back. 'Don't think I'll make any, sir. Not serious ones if that's what you're suggesting.'

This wasn't like Johnson. He was a fair man, but paternal wasn't his natural management style.

The DI sighed rubbing his jaw. 'I'm being clumsy, John. Best I tell you straight.'

'Straight is best, sir!'

'Well, then, here's the way of it. A special constable has spoken to me off the record. He told me he was there when you held Cannon down, said you were a fraction away from assaulting him, that, in his words, you'd lost it. It worried him, John.'

Niven got it now. His anger and embarrassment coalesced, colouring his cheeks to a shade of red. His mind trailed back to the moment when the special had restrained him. 'Remember who you are,' the fellow had said. Even now, those words stung because he knew that it was true, that he had lost any sense of himself and could easily have battered Cannon unmercilessly.

Johnson was looking sheepish. 'I'd like to ignore what he said, but I can't, John. He did insist he was speaking off the record, your interests at heart. In all conscience, I felt I had to follow it up, get your version.'

Niven forced himself to look the DI in the eye. The man had always been straight with him and loyal; he deserved no more than the truth, however unpalatable. It took an effort, but he told him exactly what had happened from the moment he'd entered the house, told him the special was correct, he'd been near to giving Cannon a going-over after the criminal had already surrendered to him.

'In mitigation,' he emphasized, 'I'd come close to being stabbed in the face with a junkie's needle and Cannon had a knife. My blood was up, but it was still unprofessional of me, I know.'

Johnson rubbed his face, sat back. 'Your father's long illness, your bereavement, all that strain, could have contributed, don't you think?'

Niven understood his boss was giving him an out, but he wasn't sure it really stood up as a valid excuse. How could he be sure? But it was possible, so he nodded in agreement.

'Could be, I suppose,' he said vaguely.

Johnson seemed relieved to hear him say it.

'The circumstances were extreme,' he said, like a defence counsel choosing words with careful deliberation. 'The special thought that too, said he was only mentioning this for the good of the force and yourself ... in case....'

Johnson didn't have to say 'in case it happened again'. Niven understood all right and felt his hackles rise. In his book, you didn't rat on a colleague unless there was no other choice. Maybe the special was self-serving, out for brownie points, inexperienced enough to think the book covered everything. Then again, he told himself, maybe his concerns were sincere and he was too cynical to see it.

'Are you going to suspend me, sir?' Niven said, after a silence.

'Of course not. Your actions showed great bravery in the finest traditions. I wish he hadn't told me, but it might be just as well he did. None of us is immune to stress. I want you to take two week's leave, rest and recharge your batteries. Then we'll move on, forget about all this.'

Niven figured it made sense, knew Johnson was trying to be fair. All those contrary thoughts bouncing against one another in his brain were wearying him. Perhaps he did need a rest.

'OK with me. Thank you for understanding, sir. I think I will benefit from a break.'

Johnson smiled his satisfaction. Understanding that concluded matters, Niven rose and made for the door, feeling a little light headed. Before he exited, Johnson called his name and he turned around.

'Look, John,' he said. 'Don't imagine for a minute most policemen haven't had a moment like that. You're not that naïve and neither am I. You're a good copper and the fact that you understand what happened to you is good. For God's sake, don't be too hard on yourself. It's just a blip.'

'Yes, sir. Just a blip.' Niven said. 'But what if I had let go. This would have been a very different conversation.'

Johnson frowned, nodded sagely. 'Yes, it would. But that exact combination of circumstances will never occur again and you're more aware now. It'll be a learning curve for you. Main thing is you rest. Start your leave whenever you like, except make it within the next few days.'

Niven managed a grin. 'I'll bring my paperwork in for you to finish, sir.'

'Get out of it,' Johnson called after him as he departed his office.

As soon as John Niven left his office, Johnson sighed, picked up his mobile and dialled. His call was answered on the second ring.

'It's me, 'Johnson said. 'We agreed I'd call you if the young man was causing me any concern. It's not serious, but I thought I'd keep you informed.'

'OK, Tom, let's have it.'

'You sure? Aren't you giving yourself unnecessary grief? You could just forget.'

There was a momentary silence on the other end, 'Ever make a mistake, Tom?'

Johnson laughed. 'You knew me well enough once. I'm perfect, aren't I?'

'Some mistakes – most mistakes – go away with time, Tom. Others won't. You think you've pushed them away, but they're always there. You want to put things right, but you can't. You can only watch, wait and hope for a chance.'

'I can understand, that, believe me, but don't get your hopes up, eh!'

'So tell me what's happened?'

Johnson explained about John Niven's violent altercation with Jack Cannon, the reason the special had reported him and that he'd heard Gill and he had split up.

'I could tell he was pretty shaken up but putting a brave face on it,' the D.I. added, 'so I insisted he took a couple of weeks off. Think he'll get over it, but you asked me to let you know such things, hence this call.'

'Well he's certainly got bottle. As long as he can control the aggression, he'll do. Appreciate you informing me.'

'Hope it isn't a mistake?'

'I'm following my conscience now, hoping it will tell me what to do – if the need arises.'

'It might never arise,' Johnson said. 'You're not hoping it will, are you?'

'Thought you knew me better than that. I haven't changed.'

'He'll be all right,' Johnson said. 'I know he's a detective sergeant but he's still a bit raw. I'll keep a special eye out, but no favours.'

'Thanks, pal.'

The call ended there. Johnson felt sad. He didn't like doing things behind John Niven's back, but at the same time he was a man who recognized other loyalties that went back to when he was a young man. He only hoped he was doing the right thing for all concerned, that there would be no unforeseen consequences, because if he wasn't exactly playing with fire he was edging too close to it for comfort.

CHAPTER 9

Around the same time as Niven exited Johnson's office, Alan Thompson took a deep breath and stepped out onto the school's concrete quadrangle. Immediately, his heart sank because the crowd in the far corner had already swollen. He managed to conquer his trepidation, knowing how Preston would laugh at him if he backed off. Right now, he'd probably gathered a few cronies to watch the showdown from the staff room window, might even be taking bets.

'The God squad's coming,' someone yelled.

'Belt 'em with your Bible,' another voice shouted.

That was the penalty of teaching religion to little heathens. He resisted the temptation to seek out the heretics and that encouraged others to join in the heckling.

'Watch out, watch out, there's a religious maniac about,' several voices chorused together followed by snide laughter.

His sense of failure was enhanced by each insult. They were throwing his efforts to teach them back in his face and he felt angry enough to strike out at his tormentors; it was an effort to keep in control.

At his approach, the crowd parted like the Red Sea. He was aware of an unnatural silence descending, sensation-seeking faces staring at him. They had been attracted by Tyrell doing his thing, but perhaps this was going to be even better, wet behind the ears Tommo charging into a fracas. At that moment, he regretted his decision; his anger overcame his inhibitions, though. He kept reminding himself that, in any case, he hadn't much to lose. For once, he might even do some good, make something of a mark. Better late than never.

Tyrell was slapping the smaller lad across the face repeatedly with an open hand. It was like a cameo from a silent film except each slap was obviously painful.

'Stop it!' Thomson shouted.

Tyrell swung around, just a hint of uncertainty in his face, quickly replaced by a cocky assuredness when he realized this was a teacher he didn't fear in the slightest. He smiled at his two mates who were holding the lad.

'Just a friendly play-fight, sir,' he grunted and let his gaze drift onto the crowd. 'Ask anybody. They'll tell you.'

'Get to the staff room!' Thompson ordered. He pointed at his accomplices and the lad they were holding. 'And you three as well. I'll deal with this matter there.'

Tyrell made no move, glared at the lad. 'Ask him if you don't believe me.' With menace clearly meant for his victim, he followed it up with, 'Tell the man!'

The victim looked from Tyrell to the teacher. Thompson could see in his eyes he was weighing up his future, wondering whether to take a chance and grass on Tyrell as a way out of his predicament. But he knew what that future would mean if he split. In the end, he just lowered his head.

'They were just mucking about, sir.'

'See!' Tyrell had the audacity to smile. 'All sorted. You made a mistake, sir. Teachers are always doing that and I have to fetch my old man down so often he's started wearing short trousers and bringing dinner money.'

Amused, the crowd tittered. Tyrell visibly preened. 'Your tea'll be getting cold up in the staff room,' he continued, playing up to them. 'If I was you I'd go and finish it and talk about me to all those other teachers who want to pick on me.'

Furious, Thompson stared at the youth. He could see a gleam of triumph in the recalcitrant's eyes for the way he'd reversed their roles here. The pupil was chiding the teacher, showing his power, a patronizing smile lighting up his face while he milked the moment.

Like in the old time western films climaxing with a gun fight, the critical moment had arrived and all those watching knew it. Thompson wished he'd never embarked on this course. George Preston would probably be looking down on him now like God almighty, waiting for him to back off. He imagined he could hear laughter echoing through the staff room and his face reddened. He wanted so much to walk away. Did it matter if he lost more face when he only had weeks left? He could go on the sick, couldn't he?

But there was part of him that was still resolved to win this battle, to prove to himself he wasn't the total wash-out everyone must think he was.

'Get up to the staff room,' he heard himself say through gritted teeth, surprised at the authority in his voice. As though subdued too long, all his pent up emotions seemed to burst through, ride on the words.

A low murmur arose and he knew he wasn't the only one surprised by his tone, that the spectators couldn't comprehend that this was the same teacher. Tyrell's mouth twitched. The low murmur became excited chatter. Something unexpected was occurring and the outcome of the confrontation wasn't going the way they expected.

Tyrell wasn't used to losing his audience. He sensed the change and lost the grin, his cheeks puffing out like a frog's. Then, in a slow, calculated movement, he stuck two fingers up inches from the teacher's face, turned his back and walked away, heading for the school gate.

Thompson went after him in a fury, grasped his shoulder and pulled him round. Tyrell glared at him, but there was a look of uncertainty in his eyes, the look of a bully unused to being challenged, not so sure of himself anymore.

'You can't do that,' he said, trying to push the teacher's hand off. 'That's assault.'

Thomson didn't let go and they stared at each other in a battle of wills, the teacher still furious and determined that, having come this far, he wasn't going to let the little rat best him this time.

'You tell him, Tyrell,' one of the crowd called out. 'He can't stop you.'

Tyrell's eyes flicked past the teacher to his supporters. His expression gave him away. He knew he was on the spot here, in danger of losing face. With a wriggling motion he broke free. Then, like a horse snorting, he hawked and spat at the teacher's feet.

The vulgar contempt of the action, the ugly defiance, opened the floodgates inside Thompson. In an instinctive need to retaliate, his fist drew back, hurtled forward like a piston into Tyrell's chest. The power in the blow sent the bully staggering backwards. He only just managed to retain his balance. With the crowd urging him on, his first reaction was to step forward, fists raised. But the teacher held his ground, stood there like a zombie, stiff limbed, eyes glazed, fists at the ready, nothing like the mild teacher of repute. Unsure, Tyrell hesitated for a moment, then, losing his courage, spun on his heel and headed for the gate, the jeers of his former so-called supporters following him.

In a daze, Thompson watched him go. He was conscious of his own heavy breathing. It seemed to come from deep down inside him, from another being lurking down there that had escaped its cage. He lifted his bunched fists, stared at them wondering whether they really belonged with his body. Finally, his reason returned and the implications of what he had done seeped through to his consciousness.

Amidst accompanying cheers and jeers, he started back to the staff room, aware there would be consequences. Strangely, he found he couldn't regret his actions, felt less shame than vindication. He'd done what the system had failed to do to Tyrell long ago – faced up to the bully and made him think twice.

A hushed silence greeted his return to the staff room. His head held high, he crossed the room, picked his briefcase off the chair. He was aware of George Preston's amazed expression, as though he'd just watched a dwarf metamorphose into a giant.

'If anybody wants me,' he announced to the whole room, 'which I think is highly likely, I'll be waiting in my classroom.'

He winked at Preston. 'By the way, George, I just found a cure, and it feels a damn sight better than prevention. Must have been hell for you, walking on eggs all those years.'

Back in his classroom, surprisingly calm, he read his newspaper. Nobody disturbed him until half an hour later the headmaster entered with two uniformed policemen.

'These two gentleman are here to arrest you,' the head told him, unable to hide the anger boiling underneath the words because he knew this would reflect badly on him and his school, that the festering sores under the surface might be exposed.

They led Alan Thompson out of the school in handcuffs. In defiance of their teachers' orders to come away, kids crowded open-mouthed at the windows to watch his departure. As the van pulled away, Thompson took one last lingering look at the building. Though this wasn't the way he would have chosen to leave, he felt a pleasant sense of relief that an unwelcome chapter of his life would now be behind him and he would never return to it again. Let them do their worst. He was well out of it.

CHAPTER 10

Niven decided he'd spend a day or two on his backlog of paperwork before complying with DI Johnson's instruction to take time off. He was beginning to look forward to the enforced break, though. Perhaps a change of scenery was the answer to his recent state of mind and he'd come back a new man, brain spring-cleaned, no more negative thoughts which once would have been alien to him. He'd heard it said stress could sneak up on you and you didn't recognize it until it sank its teeth in with a vengeance: that might explain a lot.

He'd just begun writing when another DS, Bob Harker, approached his desk with that cheerful look of his that made you think he was about to announce he'd won the lottery and the Boro team had won promotion on the same day. It usually meant he wanted something.

'Got a strange one in, John,' he said. 'A teacher gone native in Grove Hill. Beat up a pupil – well – hit one anyway. Same thing these days, eh! It was one of those nice Tyrells on the receiving end. Hope the teacher got his money's worth? In for a penny, in for a pound, eh!'

Niven raised an eyebrow, wondered why Harker was telling him this. 'So it was a case of role reversal! Usually the pupils beat up the teachers.'

Harker came to the point. 'We've a lot of men out on jobs, John. Need someone in on the interview with me. Wondered whether you'd step in. No need to say anything if you don't want to. Just sit there, look wise in that inimitable way of yours and make it all legal.'

Niven managed to crack a smile. 'Look wise, you say. That's a new one. Knew I was good for something. Only wise monkey living in Hartlepool, am I?'

'Talking of being wise, I met Gill and—'

Niven held up his hand, 'Don't go there, Bob!' He rose from his chair. 'Just take me to this psycho teacher of yours.'

The teacher was in the interview-room waiting for them. His physical appearance surprised Niven. Sandy haired and bespectacled – he looked innocuous. But what really struck the detective was his air of insouciance; it seemed so incongruous for an intelligent man who must realize he was in trouble. The detective had seen hardened criminals show more signs of nerves. This fellow looked as though he was ready for a pleasant chat rather than about to face a charge that could change his life. Niven wondered whether he was in denial or, failing that, had lost his marbles.

'So you've turned down a solicitor, Mr Thompson,' Bob Harker opened after he'd set the tape running and introduced himself and Niven.

'I'm perfectly capable of explaining what happened, detectives,' the teacher answered. 'I know what I did was wrong, of course I do, but, as you must be well aware in your vocation, sometimes a man can be provoked. I don't regret what I did and I know there'll be a price to pay.'

Harker glanced at his colleague, the tilt of his eyebrows making it evident that he thought they had a right one here. Niven wasn't so sure, though. The teacher seemed strange, but he had summed up his position eloquently enough.

The interview began, Harker's skillful questioning eliciting the bare facts, the teacher elaborating enough to explain how his temper had got the better of him when Tyrell had defied him and how he'd exploded when Tyrell had spat at him. Niven said little, but as the sad tale unfolded, he found himself empathizing. He recalled his own state of mind when he'd tackled Cannon. Another turn of the screw and it could easily have been him sitting on the wrong side of a table with questions being fired at him dispassionately by a disciplinary board.

'Now you know what happened,' the teacher concluded. 'But there's much more depth to it, if you're interested.'

Harker narrowed his eyes. 'The facts are what we're most interested in, Mr Thompson, not an academic treatise. You've admitted striking the lad in the way he says you did, told us the manner in which you were provoked. What else can there be?'

Thompson gave him a look that was almost pitying, as though Harker was living on another planet, couldn't understand what should have been all too palpable to a man in his position.

'In mitigation,' Thompson went on, 'I have to say I've been struggling to control the classes and resigned recently because it was getting me down. The sense of failure was very depressing. Then, just once, I decided to stand up to a bully boy – matter of pride, I suppose. Foolish in retrospect.'

Harker's tone was sharp and judgemental, 'That's your reason, is it? Your ego was offended?'

Thompson looked at him over the rim of his glasses. 'Like the police,' he said, 'the schools fail. People forget schools have their share of embryonic criminals who think they can do what they like. Reason is no use against them because they think with their emotions – not reason. When they're caught it's never their fault, always someone else's, and there are plenty of people willing to take up their cause, gloss over their misdemeanours. The police are in the same boat as I found myself in, paddling against the tide for much the same reasons.'

It was an impassioned little speech and Niven thought it contained more than a grain of truth. He found himself identifying with the sentiments because his own thoughts had been running along similar lines, making him doubt his future in the force.

'That's twice you've mentioned our line of work,' he stated, speaking for the first time. 'Any particular reason for that?'

Harker frowned, shot him a look that asked what the hell did that have to do with anything.

The teacher adjusted his spectacles, turned his blue eyes to Niven.

'My father was a policeman a long time ago so I've always had a little interest.' He gazed wistfully over the detectives' heads. 'Most policeman were given respect in those days – as were most teachers. Would that we could turn the clock back.'

There was little else to say after that. The case seemed fairly cut and dried and Harker wound the interview up, calling for a uniform who led Thompson out of the room. He thanked Niven for sitting in.

'Could tell it must have been a real bore for you when you threw that last question in to the mix,' he added. 'Almost as boring as that paperwork, I expect.'

'He'll get bail, won't he?'

'Don't see why not.' Harker shot him a quizzical glance. 'Why the interest?'

Niven sighed. 'I suppose I found a bit of truth in what he had to say. Felt a bit sorry for him actually. One moment of madness when his nerves were frayed and his whole career is down the shoot.'

'Yeah!' Harker agreed. 'But that's all it takes. All we need to know is he crossed the line. Can't get too involved in whys and wherefores or we'd be like all those mealy-mouthed social workers.'

It was a hard truth Harker espoused and Niven knew he was right. There wasn't enough space in your soul to carry around all the hard luck stories you came across. Yet, in spite of himself, he felt a kind of kinship with the teacher.

CHAPTER 11

A couple of hours after Thompson's interview, Niven finished for the day. As he strode through the foyer, he noticed the teacher sitting on a wooden bench, a burly uniform beside him. He supposed he was waiting to be called down to the custody suite to be formally charged. With an overhead light reflecting on his lenses and that strange unconcerned air that ill befitted the circumstances, he looked more like a man waiting to go on holiday, free of all burdens. In fact, Niven thought he looked a bit weird. Had his sympathy been misplaced?

'Thank you, detective,' the teacher called out as he walked past.

Perplexed, Niven halted, swung round to face him. Punters rarely thanked him. No doubt the fellow was about to release a volley of sarcasm in his direction. He waited for it, but the teacher just smiled benignly in his direction while the burly guard raised his eyebrows.

'Did I do you a favour or something?' Niven said, a hint of annoyance in his tone.

The benign smile didn't alter. 'Your silence spoke to me,' he said. 'I could feel that you were sympathetic.'

Niven gave him the eyes. He didn't like his assumption but, worse than that, its accuracy. He'd thought of himself as the inscrutable cop. Was he so transparent, then? If he was, he must be slipping.

'One of those pretend psychics, are you?' he grunted, eyes sliding to the guard who seemed to be taking no notice at all.

Thompson shook his head. 'Don't be offended. Surviving in a school sharpens your instincts a bit. You need to know what's coming, have to reads pupils quickly – anticipate. Sometimes that extends to adults. I apologize if I presumed wrongly.'

Niven didn't know how to answer. The guy had spooked him. 'Get yourself a solicitor,' he said, not unkindly.

As he exited the building lost in thought he almost bumped into someone coming through the door. He started to apologize, then realized it was Gill. What was she doing here?

She pushed her wind-blown hair into place, looked him up and down as though she was measuring him for a new suit.

'Well, I can see you're OK,' she said, sounding annoyed. 'On the outside at least.'

He recovered his wits, said. 'Why shouldn't I be?'

Gill explained she'd had a call at work, a man who wouldn't give his name telling her Niven had been involved in a dangerous situation and might need her support, that she shouldn't desert him in his hour of need.

'You look fine to me!' she concluded and he could tell she was embarrassed and annoyed simultaneously. 'So someone was making mischief.'

'You've no idea who it was?'

She shook her head. 'No, but whoever it was knew where I worked. So it was all made up, was it?'

Niven shrugged. 'There was an incident, but as you can see I'm perfectly OK – on the outside as you say. Whoever he is, the guy's out of date.' He sighed. 'Likely its some office gossip. If it happens again, we can put a trace on.'

An awkward silence followed, then Niven said, 'Look, would you like to go for a drink.'

She held up a hand like a policewoman on duty. 'Best not,' she said. 'Sorry my concern was … misplaced.'

'Thanks anyway,' he muttered, wishing it didn't sound so hollow. 'Sorry for your trouble.'

Gill waited for a moment, as though she was expecting or

hoping for him to say something else, then turned on her heel.

'See you!' she called over her shoulder as she marched out of the door.

Just before he followed her out, he noticed Alan Thompson staring at him. He waited a moment to let Gill get away then exited himself. The prospect of two weeks off was pleasing, but he realized he would be alone. Last year around this time he'd been on holiday in Greece with Gill. As a teacher, her holidays were fixed but he'd managed to wangle it so his leave coincided with her break and they'd had a relaxed holiday in the sun. Alan Thompson, he supposed, would be due his holidays soon, but being on bail with his future ruined would take the edge right off his enjoyment.

CHAPTER 12

Fraser Jackson, small time arms dealer, owed money, otherwise he wouldn't have been lurking in the sand dunes at Seaton Carew with the cold north-east wind blowing in off the grey sea ruffling his jacket, flapping at his trousers and generally abusing and irritating him.

Swirls of sand scratching at his eyes didn't alter his focus from the man walking along the deserted beach towards him for even a second; he was aware this was a new source of money. The guy had walked up to him in the pub three nights ago, calm as you like and warned him the police were going to raid his home – that he'd better move his guns to another place. Then he'd walked off leaving Fraser so bemused at his audacity he hadn't even gone after him.

He'd moved the weapons within the hour and the next day the police had raided, smirking like they knew the secret of life. As they left empty handed, it was he who was smirking and the pigs looking like they were bacon. The following night, the mystery guy had walked in to the pub again, told him now that he'd proved he could trust him, he wanted to buy two handguns. Fraser, cautious of a guy he didn't know, agreed with the proviso that the delivery should be in two parts. Last night, in this same spot the guy had come up with the readies for one of the guns and ammunition. Tonight they were meeting for the second exchange.

Fraser felt more comfortable with it now, guessed lady luck was smiling on him. This guy, whoever he was, had proved to be his saviour, not only that, had increased his cashflow just when his mistress was starting to complain they hadn't gone away to Spain for Easter as they usually did. Now, though Easter was past, he had enough to take her away and to keep her happy for a few more months. By then he would probably be tiring of the mercenary bitch anyway.

The guy came through the dunes to the spot where he stood, halted a yard away, the wind behind him so that the sleeves of his loose coat billowed, creating an illusion he had large biceps under the material. In reality, he was decidedly average in build. Fraser, in fact, hadn't done business with anyone like him before. That educated voice, that blond haired, blue eyed look seemed too angelic compared to the hard men he normally sold to whose faces betrayed a streak of resentment at their lot in life.

This guy looked more like a clerk or a schoolteacher: cerebral more than physical. Strangely, as part of the deal, he'd had to show him how to load and fire the gun. Yet, despite those anomalies, Fraser had to admit there was a certainty about him, an impression that nothing would divert him from whatever cause drove him. The fact he'd known about that raid remained a mystery. He'd refused to reveal his source, but Fraser, only too grateful, hadn't pressed it.

'Got my package, then,' the guy asked Fraser, the last burst of the evening sun forming a halo around his blond head.

Fraser felt inside his jacket, withdrew a weapon wrapped in cellophane.

'Got my money?' he riposted.

The guy pulled a package from his pocket. They exchanged, then opened their respective packages. Fraser ripped away two layers of newspaper. He was anticipating enough money to help him out of his troubles but found only an empty toilet roll.

'What the—'

Bafflement gave way to terrified understanding as he watched the gun he'd sold the previous night suddenly appear in the stranger's hand, heard the words coming at him through the wind.

'I believe in recycling, Fraser. Even dead toilet rolls have their uses so maybe there's hope for you. Food for the fish is one idea that springs to mind.'

Struggling to control himself, the arms-dealer voiced his first thought, his voice trembling.

'You're a copper! It's all been a set-up.'

The guy shook his head. 'Not too bright, are we? Would a copper warn you then go to all this trouble?'

Fraser narrowed his eyes. If the guy wasn't a copper what was he? A thought colder than that persistent north east wind swept through him. Was he sent by men he owed money?

'I can get money,' he stuttered. 'There's things I can sell ... just need time.'

'Not after money! It's just a case of simple economics. I had enough money for one gun, not for a second. This way I get two for one.'

Relief surged through Fraser, but lasted only as long as it took to re-focus on that gun. 'Why me?' he whined, fighting down his panic.

The blue eyes seemed to be laughing as they lifted to the darkening heavens.

'Oh, the irony of it all,' he exclaimed. 'When trouble comes that's the perennial question, isn't it?' He glared at Fraser. 'Shouldn't you be asking, "Why not me?" You haven't done much in life to deserve mercy, have you?'

Fraser, convinced now he was in the presence of a mad man, sank to his knees and lowered his head.

'Please don't kill me,' he pleaded, tears in his eyes.

Blue eyes laughed again. 'Don't worry, I've got what I want. There's no need for me to kill you. Someone will one day, for sure.'

When Fraser looked up, he was already walking away. The arms-dealer remained on his knees until there was a safe distance between them, then, cursing his luck, rose to his feet, cupped his hands around his mouth and yelled after the figure silhouetted against the setting sun.

'I'll get you, you bastard. Nobody does one on Fraser Jackson and gets away with it.'

Carried on the wind, the words reached their target. Blue eyes smiled and kept walking, entranced by the expanse of black sea on one side, the dome of dark sky above, wondering at the mysterious cycles of the universe as, with slow majesty, day turned into night. Knowing what he knew, Fraser's threat was as inconsequential to him as one of the grains of sand beneath his feet.

CHAPTER 13

Two nights after the business on Seaton Carew beach, the blond, blue eyed man was ready to begin his quest. From now on, until his business was concluded, he would forget who he was, think of himself as PC 49; that would become his alter ego. He liked the sound of it because it brought back childhood memories, a time of solid certainties in his life. He sighed. How times changed!

The uniform fitted him quite well. Though it was old, it was lovingly preserved and he'd brought it up to date. Wearing it now, he felt he'd grown a new skin, cast off the old one which was virtually finished anyway. It made him walk taller, made him stronger, more resolute than his other, defeated self.

Respect! It had been in short supply in his life recently, but now he could almost sense it in the air as he strode through the shopping parade with his shoulders squared, right in the role. Yes! In spite of everything, respect was still there for a copper when he walked amongst the public. He could see it in the eyes of the passers by, in the way they cleared a path for him. Should teachers wear uniforms, he wondered, idly? Of course, he was aware it had to do with power as well, maybe guilt too, as though a uniform gave one the ability to see everybody's hidden secrets.

Today he was going to do all these folk a favour, fulfill a destiny he should have foreseen years ago, his long neglected mission. His father was beside him, in spirit if not in the flesh. He'd be smiling his approval because this was going to be for him.

He arrived at his destination, a block of flats four storeys high just beyond the parade. The building was well maintained, neat, nothing like the part of Boro where the man he'd come for used to live. To reside here, in the village of Marton, you needed money. You could tell that by the new cars parked in the road, the way the people were dressed. Nothing wrong with improving your station in life, your milieu. Of course there wasn't! In most people it was commendable. How you did it, though; that was what counted. The man, no – correction – the scavenging beast he was here for, hadn't done it right, didn't deserve to walk these clean pavements. Walking in the sewer would have been a step up for him. His name was Jimmy Peacock and he was Terry Brannigan's erstwhile colleague in crime.

He'd selected this time of day because the other inhabitants of the flats would be at work, while his target, who kept his own hours, would still be lying in his pit of iniquity. As he went up the stairs, he could hear his breathing accelerate, knew it wasn't just from the effort, but from anticipation and excitement. In truth, he felt revivified.

He knocked on the door, had a moment of doubt as he looked through the eye hole. Supposing Peacock had changed his routine? That was hard to believe though because he was sure the fates were with him, that this was meant to be.

Sounds carried from behind the door, a chain scraping, bolts being drawn and he knew everything was as it should be. A round face, red veined like a habitual boozer's, and topped by a mop of dishevelled hair, peered through the open door. Sleep laden eyes peered out at him, travelled his length. A hand stifled a yawn calculated to convey how unimpressed its owner was by a police uniform.

'What's the story in Balamory,' a gravelly voice asked, the screwed up face and reference to the title of the children's TV programme a twin salvo to belittle his visitor. 'Guess I must be slipping well down the order when they send a uniform to my door in daylight.'

'Morning, Jimmy Peacock,' PC 49 said, cheerfully. 'The story's a long one, but if I tell you the hero's Bob Thompson you might remember it. You should remember it!'

Peacock frowned, nonplussed. Then, suddenly it came back to him. Remembrance was right there in his eyes. His visitor saw it and before he could say anything, shoulder-charged him in the chest catapulting him backwards. He stumbled, fell and, when he looked up from the floor, the constable had shut the door and was standing over him pointing a gun in his face. His whole body flinched. Instinctively, he brought his hands up.

PC 49 waited until the hands slid away to reveal the gangster's face. Peacock stared into the gun barrel, then at the man holding it, a whole gamut of emotions reflecting in his eyes. Finally, when the constable didn't pull the trigger, a glimmer of hope came into those same eyes and he stammered out his best effort.

'You're not a copper, are you? Whoever's paying you I'll pay more.'

PC 49 shook his head. 'Money! Money! Money! This isn't about money. It's about justice. Justice for Bob Thompson.' He pushed the gun into the criminal's eye, twisted the barrel like a corkscrew. 'Tell me you remember everything or I'll shoot it out, then the other one.'

'I remember, but it wasn't me!' Peacock squealed. 'I was there but it ...'

The gun lifted away from his eye socket before he finished the sentence and, just for a moment, he looked relieved. But he'd said enough to condemn himself and the gun exploded sending a bullet into the middle of his forehead. As though he'd been caught on the end of a sharp punch, his head jerked backwards and hit the floor. On his forehead, like a poppy in a bed of white snow, a flower of blood burgeoned from the bullet hole, seemed to grow into life rather than to signify the end of one. Blood trickled down his cheeks in rivulets as his wide, staring eyes seemed to concentrate on horizons beyond this life.

PC 49 had never killed before, but he had no compunction about this, only a satisfying sense of completion, a job done, justice served. In his mind's eye, he could see his dead father nodding his head, congratulating him, asking why he'd taken so long to avenge him. He wanted something to mark the event that signified something shared with his father so, hiding the gun under his tunic, he slid the card he'd printed with the number 49 from his pocket, flicked it onto the floor beside the body. Then, he stepped out of the flat leaving the door ajar.

His luck held. Once again, the stairs were deserted. On the second floor, he paused next to a radiator, stretched his arm down behind it, pulled out the coat, flat cap and plastic bag he'd hidden there the previous night. He slipped on the coat and cap and, carrying his police headgear in the plastic bag, continued his descent.

This time he used the back entrance, crossed the back yard and exited through the wooden gate. There was no road, only a narrow pathway running alongside a park. The park's tall fence and a profusion of trees and bushes hid the flats from prying eyes. With a feeling of elation, he strolled back to his car, enjoying the fresh air. It was good to feel you had nothing to lose, no need for inhibitions which could make a coward out of a man.

As he drove home, his mind turned to the other two monsters on his agenda. Since they were ensconced in Stockton Prison, they would present a much greater problem for him than Peacock had. How could he solve that one? He didn't have all the time in the world to find a solution because the clock was against him. Yet, when your purpose was clear and the spirit of your father was calling out to you, he truly believed it was possible to move mountains.

CHAPTER 14

Niven parked in front of the shops and started walking towards the flats. He felt a little better after his holiday. Though he wasn't a walker, most days he'd gone to the Yorkshire Moors, ambled a few miles, figuring the wide open spaces might change his perspective on his life and career.

It had been good to get away from the bustle of the town and the parasites he dealt with daily who sucked the blood out of decent people and didn't give a damn. Even while breathing the fresh moorland air, though, he hadn't been able to get away from himself. The lonely expanses of the Moors, with their own mysteries, increased his curiosity about his own origins. Instead of losing himself in their vastness, he wondered more and more who had brought him into this world. He asked himself time and again why it mattered in the great scheme of things: he wondered whether it was pure conceit on his part? But thinking didn't help.

The flats were cordoned off and police vans had parked up. Members of the SOCO team buzzed around in pristine white suits as though they were actors making a film to advertise the latest brand of washing powder. He spotted DI Johnson leaning against a van, taking a huge bite out of a Mars bar. He nodded as Niven approached him and pointed the Mars bar like a gun.

'Reality bites back, eh, Niv! Only just back and you're into a murder case.'

Niven gazed at the flats. 'Not many murders in Marton are there, sir? What was it? Robbery gone wrong?'

'I wish! The corpse is Jimmy Peacock, known felon from way back, man and boy. Shot in the head and gone the way of all flesh.'

'Yeah! Heard of him. He must have friends in the criminal fraternity. Ears to the ground and questions to the right people might get results.'

Johnson took another bite from the Mars bar, rolled his tongue around his lips to gather a piece trying to escape from the side of his mouth.

'My first thoughts too, but not so sure now.'

Niven stepped aside as a police photographer swept past him and entered the building.

'We've got to be careful with this,' the DI continued, his face more severe now. 'Two members of the public have already informed us they saw a police constable enter the flats around the time forensics are estimating Peacock was killed.'

'The constable didn't call it in?'

Johnson stuffed the Mars wrapper in his pocket. 'No, that was the woman from the flat opposite. She noticed the door was ajar when she came in from work last night, didn't think too much about it until it was still like that this morning. She investigated and threw up her breakfast when she saw our man on the hall floor with a bullet hole in his head.'

'What about the crime scene? Anything tasty there, apart from the woman's full fry, that is?'

Johnson sighed. 'A button from a police tunic, muddy footprints from standard issue police boots and a card on the body with the number 49 printed on it. We'll have the bullet, of course, but it'll only be useful as evidence if we find the gun and its owner.'

Niven whistled through his teeth. 'So it really could be one of our own – out for revenge – or off his trolley....'

Johnson grimaced. 'Or preferably someone making it look like one of our own.'

If one of their own had indeed gone Rambo, Niven knew the

press would be all over this one and not just the local press. An army of journalists would poke grubby fingers into every nook and cranny. Walking on eggs wouldn't be in it. The brass would be apoplectic and the pressure would cascade downwards to the coal-face.

'That number 49 mean anything to you,' Johnson asked. ''Cos I haven't a clue.'

Niven frowned.'Gold Rush in the Yukon in 1849. Charlie Chaplin made a film about it. The miners were called the forty niners.' He shook his head. 'Doesn't ring any bells, sir.'

'It's obviously a calling card, the kind serial killers leave.'

'You mean like in the movies the killer's throwing a gauntlet down, tantalizing us with a hint, telling us to work it out if we're clever enough.'

'If so, he's been watching too many episodes of Morse,' Johnson said dolefully. 'Must think all coppers are cerebral types and like crosswords and cryptic clues. Doesn't know what simple souls we are.'

Someone inside the building called Johnson's name. That was followed by another urgent voice requesting his presence.

The DI grunted. 'And so it begins!'

'You're the man of the moment now, sir,' Niven said. 'What do you want me to do?'

'We've got teams of uniforms and detectives on the way. You can supervise a house to house. I'll send DS Thomas out here to help. He'll bring you right up to speed before you brief the men.'

Johnson started for the door, but paused on the threshold. 'Got to ask. Don't want to make a big thing of it – you're OK, aren't you?'

'Refreshed,' Niven said, without elaborating, figuring his problems were too personal and he'd have to get on with his work. 'Thanks for your concern, sir. It's appreciated.'

Minutes later Thomas came out and greeted Niven. He was a talkative Welshman, a good man. Together they looked at maps of the area, decided on areas they'd cover, the lines the questioning should take. When the men arrived, they briefed them and set them to work, taking a few buildings themselves.

At the end of a tedious day that yielded little, they arrived back at HQ for the wash-up. Johnson was already in the incident room in a huddle with the silver haired and spruce Detective Chief Inspector Snaith. When their confab was finished, the DI came over to speak to Thomas and Niven. Niven thought his boss already looked harassed.

'Make my day and tell me you got something useful.'

DS Thomas summed it up. 'The police constable was noticed mainly because people don't see many on foot in the area, but descriptions are sketchy. We checked with the uniforms and they didn't have a man out there. Someone saw him entering the building but no one reports him leaving, so we think he went out the back way where it's quiet. He was caught on one CCTV camera near the shops but it's only a fleeting sideways glimpse and the image is grainy.'

Johnson pulled thoughtfully at his two chins, his eyes flitting between the two detectives.

'If the uniforms didn't know he was on that patch, he could be a fake,' he stated, a trace of optimism in his voice making clear this was a preferred option.

Thomas glanced at Niven. 'Plenty of those around, eh, boyo! Worked with them, I have.'

Unamused, Johnson gave him a stare and continued. 'Could have dressed up to gain entry. Nobody questions a bobby.'

'On the other hand,' Thomas said. 'Maybe he's just someone with a uniform fetish, gets a kick out of the sense of power it gives him. Bit like dressing up in the Boro strip and thinking you're the real article – there's eleven do that on Saturdays by the way.'

Niven thought he detected something in the DI's eyes, a preoccupation with other thoughts.

'Something you're not telling us, sir?'

Johnson ran a hand through his mane of grey hair and sighed. 'Peacock had turned police informer, was tantalizing us with tit-bits, but kept promising serious stuff.'

Niven vibrated his bottom lip with a finger. 'So it's possible someone found out about Peacock gobbing off,' he ventured. 'Got scared and our policeman, or pretend policeman, was a hitman sent to eliminate him.'

'If so, the uniform was a piece of pure cheek,' Thomas added, 'intended to send out the message to all and sundry that it doesn't pay to hunt with the hounds and run with the hares.'

Niven could see it that way too, but thought they were getting too far ahead of themselves. Too many pieces didn't fit for him, so he spoke up.

'On the other hand, our hitman walked right through that shopping parade, in broad daylight and in uniform. Not exactly the way a professional would act. More like an exhibitionist enjoying himself. Then, there's the mysterious calling card. Why did he leave it? What's its significance?'

Johnson made a face. 'For sure, we've a long way to go with this. We can't prejudge too much. Let's just hope he isn't one of ours.'

Niven caught his boss's worried look, tried to assuage it with a crumb of comfort.

'Could be just a proper nutter with a uniform fetish like Thomas suggested, picking on an old gangster for the kudos he believes it carries.'

'Only in Hollywood,' Johnson stated, shaking his head. 'Only in Hollywood.'

The rest of the team drifted in. Niven could see from their faces it had been a long day for them too, with little by way of reward. The banter was non-existent. Johnson, sensing their weariness, kept his wash-up as short as possible so they could get off home.

As he drove off in darkness, Niven ran his mind over what

they knew. Peacock's record apparently showed episodes of violence stretching way back. He'd done time for two robberies, but had been a main suspect in others of a more serious nature without the investigating officers coming up with enough proof to nail him. Terry Brannigan and John Paxton had been his usual conspirators and both were currently in prison. How a scum bag parasite like Peacock ended up in a respectable place like Marton was another question; it seemed the equivalent of a rottweiler sharing a kennel with poodles. The revelation that he had turned informer was puzzling. Possibly, at his age, he'd given up crime, but found greed hadn't given up on him and he wanted to squeeze the last pips out of the orange, make a bit more money out of his criminal knowledge without risking any more jail time. For sure, greed was the usual driving force with men like him and what finally brought them down.

Later, lying in bed in his Hartlepoool flat, questions he hoped to avoid returned to plague him. Did he really want to spend his days looking for this murderer who, truth be told, he considered had done the civilized world a favour by ridding it of scum like Jimmy Peacock, a career criminal who had laughed at the law all his life and now, in death, would have all its resources seeking his murderer? He knew it was a sentiment hardly fitting for an investigating officer who needed to observe strict neutrality. His sympathies seemed to be rather too flexible these days. He'd felt guilty about the strange affinity he'd felt with that schoolteacher a few weeks back. Driven to exasperation by a wild kid who should have been restrained long ago, did he deserve to pay such a high price for his misdemeanour? Niven considered he'd done his job professionally today, but he was still in doubt where his future lay, had merely suppressed feelings and doubts which needed to be resolved.

CHAPTER 15

Gill drove through the St Hild's area of Middlesbrough, the old centre from which the infant Hercules had spread as the fastest growing town in the country when iron ore had been discovered in the nearby Eston hills. She negotiated a maze of streets, emerged onto a stretch of land deserted except for a handful of sad, isolated buildings which were so ramshackle and desolate they looked like the last outposts of pre-war Middlesbrough. In the near distance, the Riverside Stadium – that magnificent temple of optimism, home to Middlesbrough Football Club – hovered over the landscape like an alien flying saucer ready to launch an attack on a town that burdened it with too many high expectations.

She felt like an alien in a strange land herself right now. What was she doing here? It wasn't like her to interfere in other people's business, but she'd already started something and she thought she might be able to finish it. Anyway, John Niven, whom she was hoping to help, wasn't just other people, was he?

She was doing this for him, had spent the weeks since their break up on it because she didn't think he'd do it for himself and her instincts told her it was something he needed. If it could possibly help him with his current state of mind, it was surely worth a try. It might bring them back together in the long run, but that wasn't her motivation. She saw this as doing her best to help someone she cared about, always would, in spite of the fact he'd hurt her.

The car bumped down the cobbled road. Eventually, she

spotted what she was looking for, an old warehouse with the name 'Brannigan Scaffolding' painted on it. The fact it seemed to be in the middle of nowhere concerned her. The nearest building to it, equally forbidding, was forty yards away. She told herself not to be so girly; she'd come this far so she might as well drive down the rough dirt road to take a closer look.

She parked close to the building, pretty sure, given the rusted metal shutter over the entrance and the huge lock and chain, it was going to be a wasted trip. On closer inspection, though, she noticed there was a small door built into the shutter and supposed there was a chance she could gain entry there. With its rundown look, she'd have bet the building was disused, possibly due for demolition like others in the area which had become eyesores.

She got out of the car, walked up to the building. When she pushed the small door, it shuddered open, surprising her. Without gaining any response, she called out several times. Then, deciding she'd come this far, so might as well go for broke, she stepped inside.

The interior was like a huge cave, spacious and gloomy. Overhead a gallery ran all the way round the walls. What little light there was, sneaked through dust smeared windows set high in the roof. At floor level, stalls set against the walls contained lengths of scaffolding. As Gill advanced indistinct shapes loomed at the edges of her vision, played on her imagination, making her uncertain about what she was doing. She thought about retreating but, reprimanding herself for allowing her imagination to run riot, got a grip on her nerve and advanced.

A fluttering sound up above set her heart pounding and she instinctively ducked. When she straightened and looked up, she saw the culprits were two pigeons perched on a beam craning their necks in her direction like two fussy housewife's curious about a new neighbour. One flapped its wings and cooed softly as though welcoming her. Smiling, Gill pressed on.

A little further in she heard a more sinister sound, a mewling this time. It only lasted a second but she was almost sure it came from a cat. Likely there was more than one feline living here to keep the mice down. Possibly they'd had a scrap and the loser was complaining. Deciding it was best ignored, she pressed on but could see no sign of human presence and received no response on those occasions she called out.

She was ready to give up when she spotted a small cabin abutting the wall at the far end. If anyone was about they could well be inside and couldn't hear her shouts. However, unless business was so poor they were saving on electricity, she'd have expected to see some light behind the cabin's small window.

When she was ten yards from the cabin, that same mewling started again, this time louder and more distinct. It sent a cold chill through her body because it sounded more human than animal, conveying a profound agony, pitiful to hear. A warning instinct told Gill not to look, but a perverse fascination compelled her to swivel her head in the direction of the sound.

At first, she couldn't comprehend what she saw, thought her mind was playing tricks. But it was no illusion. At the level of her eyes were two bloodied bare legs, nothing supporting them, as though someone were taking a stroll in mid-air. Just for a moment, she thought she was seeing a ghost on a different physical plane to her own. Then, when she hauled her eyes upwards, what she saw it was all too real. A half-naked man, his torso covered in bloody weals, was hanging in chains from a high beam in one of the stalls. Her first instinct was to run, but pitiful eyes pleading from a battered and swollen face rooted her to the spot.

She knew she had to try to help this man, couldn't leave him like that. But how to get him down? Peering through the gloom, she noticed two large, dark, circular shapes like big round eyes balanced on tall stalks. Wires snaked from behind the eyes all the way to the cabin. Gill's stomach muscles contracted as it dawned on her the huge eyes were in fact searchlights. What if those searchlights suddenly came on? Whoever had done this terrible thing could still be around? What if they were watching her now! It was enough to make her change her mind about staying. It would do neither the tortured man nor her any good if she was caught, would it? Far better to ring John for help. It wouldn't take long for him to get help here.

Backing away, she fumbled in her pocket for her mobile, started to dial. John answered on the second ring. She'd never been more pleased to hear his voice.

'I'm at Brannigan's Scaffolding, John,' she said, her voice just above a whisper, 'It's a warehouse. There's a man—'

White light! Dazzling! An Arctic storm bombarding her vision, wiping out everything, numbing the senses, leaving only panic. Blinded and confused, she dropped the phone. Even as it slipped from her fingers, a hollow feeling invaded the pit of her stomach. That phone was a lifeline. Now it was gone she was cut off from the outside world. Whoever had turned on the searchlights, if they hadn't already detected her presence, couldn't miss her standing there like an actress with stage fright.

Suddenly, as though a creature had manifested from another dimension where nightmares reside, a black shape intervened between her and the light. Impaled on her fear, Gill couldn't move her legs. The creature took human form and she saw that it was holding a piece of scaffolding. Released from her thrall, she spun away, started to run, stumbled, lost a desperate struggle for balance.

The scaffolding struck the back of her skull. Behind her eyes, a universe of stars exploded. Then, in less than the blink of an eye, a black torrent extinguished the stars.

CHAPTER 16

Niven held the phone away from his ear, stared at it as though it was a miraculous, new invention. Gill's voice had suddenly died leaving him mystified. The few words she'd spoken seemed strained, hadn't sounded like her at all. Worse though, he'd detected fear in that short communiqué, a fear she was trying to subdue. Brannigan's Scaffolding! That's what she'd said. He could only think of one Brannigan family he knew, but guessed there could be others and hoped against hope there were.

Lost in thought, wondering about that call, he didn't alter his puzzled expression as DC Short approached his desk. He couldn't think why Gill would be in a warehouse. But it was her tone of voice that really worried him – and that final, truncated phrase, 'There's a man—!' Something in the way she'd said it chilled him to the bone.

'White sands, blue sea, pretty girls … mermaids?'

Niven had been only half aware anyway. Now he looked up at Short with a vacant expression.

'What?'

'Way you were staring, thought your head had gone off on holiday,' Short said, eyeing him quizzically. 'We've a briefing in five minutes. Better get off that plane and hit the runway, sir.'

'You heard of Brannigan Scaffolding?'

'Yeah, sure! Sometimes take a short cut to the Boro match and pass right by it. Belongs to that criminal family, doesn't it? My mate arrested the father there a few years back. The father's in the nick and the place has gone down the shute. Probably it's just a front for other activities.'

Niven felt a hand had reached into his chest, clutched at his heart, tried to yank it out in one go. He was certain Gill wouldn't be in a place like that voluntarily. After what Short had just said, he was convinced she'd been calling him for help and hadn't managed to complete the call because something nasty had happened to prevent her doing so.

Aware that he could already have wasted precious time, he sprang out of his chair, caught hold of Short's arm and, before the DC could protest, guided him towards the door. The speed of the movement attracted the attention of others in the incident room.

'What's got into you?' Short said. 'You want the last waltz you should ask properly. People will talk, sir.'

'Forget the briefing, 'Niven snapped at him. 'Urgent matter! It won't wait! My decision, so my responsibility!'

As he drove the car away from HQ, Niven explained that he was sure Gill was in danger, that he needed Short to get him to Brannigan's Warehouse. Short told him no worries, that he knew short cuts, would get him there in twenty minutes. But Niven did worry. In twenty minutes, anything could have happened.

CHAPTER 17

PC 49 stood in the shadow of a nearby building, binoculars raised, watching the woman drive right up to the warehouse as though she was a tourist visiting a National Trust building instead of the criminal hangout he knew it to be. When she got out, he recognized the red hair, knew he'd seen her before at police headquarters with DS Niven. He was pretty sure she wasn't police herself so what was she doing here?

He'd been trailing Don Paxton's brother, Billy the Whizz, observing his activities and his drug deals. His plan was to befriend him, worm his way into his confidence and persuade him to take him to visit Paxton in jail under the pretence of wanting a contact inside. The idea was he'd kill Brannigan as soon as he was released, which wouldn't be far off, then kill Paxton after that during a prison visit. Of course, he wouldn't be able to walk out of the prison afterwards, but that wouldn't matter at all given his situation.

He'd followed Billy and Darren Brannigan here out of curiosity, wondering what was going on between them. Now, the woman's appearance was a surprise factor in the equation – a puzzling one. She seemed unfamiliar with her surroundings, her body language conveying uncertainty. Just as he thought she'd decided the place was deserted and intended to walk away, she pushed the small door open and stepped inside.

The temptation became too great. He sprinted across the intervening ground and edged his way around the building until he found a rusted metal fire escape that led up to a door near the roof level. Testing each rung before he used it, he climbed up.

The door was stiff through disuse but he was able to force it open. He stepped inside, found himself on a wooden gallery which had seen better days but held his weight. He couldn't see much at floor level because it was so dark. For a moment he was tempted just to let it go. What stopped him was a feeling that the woman was a lamb walking into a wolf's lair. For him to leave without making sure she was safe wouldn't be the act of a good citizen, and he didn't consider he was anything like those he was hunting.

A sudden explosion of white light seared across his vision, momentarily blinding him. When he opened his eyes, he saw the woman twenty feet below. She was standing in a circle of light and seemed totally disorientated. He noticed something else just where the light gave way to shadow. A figure suspended in chains!

He'd hardly had time to take in the scene when Darren Brannigan stepped into the light holding a length of scaffolding. It was like watching a dramatic scene in the theatre from the gallery seats, except the aggressor was no actor and the woman's fear of him wasn't manufactured. She turned and tried to run but she never had a chance. As the metal came down hard on her head PC49 flinched. Then, angered at the sheer brutality of that action, he made for the steps that led down to the body of the warehouse.

As soon as his feet touched the floor he drew his gun, yelled out and sprinted into the circle of light. Darren Brannigan, standing over the woman's prone body, the scaffolding raised as though he intended to do more damage, spun round, his mouth agape. He looked ready to launch himself at the intruder but the gun and a sense of self preservation were powerful inhibitors and he settled for glaring at the stranger who had appeared from nowhere.

'You got real style, just like your old man,' PC 49 said, forcing himself to contain his anger. His eyes leapfrogged to the hanging man, saw the bloodied face of Billy Paxton looking back at him. 'He'd approve of torture and beating a woman, your old man.'

'You're a copper,' Darren grunted, eyes wandering now as though he expected more coppers to emerge at any moment from wherever this one had crawled from.

PC49 smiled. He liked to think of himself as a copper. After all, he was doing their work for them, wasn't he? Pity he wasn't wearing the uniform today.

'That's Don Paxton's brother,' he said, pointing at the hanging man. 'History just goes on repeating itself, doesn't it? Like Don, he hangs about in all the wrong places and with all the wrong people.'

Darren narrowed his eyes. Who was this innocuous-looking idiot brandishing a gun at him and making pathetic jokes? With that blonde hair and blue eyes, that soft voice, surely he couldn't be a copper.

'You're not a copper!' he ventured.

'Nope! Got more power than a copper, Darren. The power to administer my own form of justice. Coppers have their hands tied, don't they? Maybe if they hadn't you wouldn't have come to this.'

With that, he aimed the gun low and pulled the trigger. Darren went down holding his groin and started wailing from pain and the sight of blood spilling out onto his leg. His wailing and Billy's whimpering panicked the pigeons so that they took off from their perch with a flapping that sounded like applause. PC 49 grimaced; he didn't like zoos and this was beginning to sound like one.

Darren Brannigan looked up at him, his face twisted. Any semblance of bravado had left him and his eyes were pleading.

'Don't kill me, man!' he groaned.

'Got questions,' PC said, standing closer to him. 'Want

answers. A lot depends on the answers. Catch my drift as they say?'

Darren nodded. If he played along with this crazy loon, kept him happy, there might be a chance he'd let him live.

'First question. Why did you torture our friend?'

Darren swallowed hard, hesitated. A kick aimed at his wounded groin soon reminded him where his best interests lay and that this wasn't a time to think about loyalties, only self preservation.

'My father wanted pictures sent to him in Stockton Prison – to his phone,' he groaned.

PC frowned. 'Starting a new art form appreciation amongst the criminal fraternity, is he? Something the youngsters can aspire to when they get too old for happy slapping?'

'Don Paxton's in jail shooting his mouth off. My father wants it stopped.' He nodded at Billy. 'He's using his brother there as an example – what can happen to grasses.'

PC 49 snapped his fingers. 'Phone! Give!'

Wincing with the effort, the wounded man slid his hand into his trouser pocket, pulled out his mobile and handed it over. PC 49 found the video and watched it until he'd seen enough to confirm Darren's version of events.

PC shook his head. 'The Gestapo would have been so proud of you, Darren,' he said, then shot him between the eyes.

Next he turned his attention to the woman. Leaning over her prone body, he noticed a trickle of blood running from the corner of her mouth onto her lips and chin, as though she'd miscued badly with her lipstick. She was still breathing, though, but obviously in a bad way. She might not have long left to live even if help came soon.

He stooped to pick up the mobile lying near her body, rang 999, gave the operator the location, told her a male was injured and a female close to expiring. Then, satisfied he'd done his duty, he made his exit and walked back to the derelict building where he'd parked his car.

Ten minutes later he was in the centre of Middlesbrough. His only real regret was that he hadn't worn his uniform when he'd done the business today, but there was no way he could have known he'd be called to duty because of the woman. Killing Brannigan's son hadn't been part of the plan, but he would look at it as a little bonus for the good citizens: one more bastard taken off the streets before he could do more damage. The real downside was that Don Paxton's brother might need some recovery time. That could delay, even scupper, his plans. All he could do was wait and see, explore alternatives.

He was about to drive home when he realized he had the two mobile phones with him, Darren Brannigan's and the woman's. Scrolling through the latter, he found John Niven's name listed, decided he might as well give him a call.

CHAPTER 18

The ring tone irritated Niven with its persistence, like an itch he couldn't scratch. The journey was already taking longer than Short's estimation owing to a spate of heavy traffic, and he had other things on his mind as he sped through the streets of Middlesbrough, DC Short at his side helping with directions. Then he noticed it was Gill's number flashing and pulled over. Perhaps his imagination had got the better of him earlier and she was calling now to tell him everything was OK.

He hurled his voice into the phone. 'Gill! Is that you?'

'Your woman's in a bad way,' a muffled voice responded. 'I've sent the emergency services to her.'

Those words were like an arrow to his heart. If he'd been concerned before, his concern shot up the scale now.

'Who is this? What do you mean?'

'You'll be hearing about it in due course,' the voice informed him.

Niven tried to keep control, failed. 'If you've hurt her—'

'I saved her!' The caller's indignation wasn't disguised. 'I had to shoot a man to do it. I think some common courtesy from you wouldn't be amiss.'

Niven bunched his free hand into a fist, forced himself to keep calm, tone down the aggression in his voice. No matter his heart was bursting, it was best to humour this lunatic, whoever he was, if he had information about Gill.

'How'd you get this number?'

'I'm using her phone, of course. As I've made clear, she's in no state to call you.'

'Where is she?'

'Brannigan's Warehouse. Its doubling as a slaughter house at the moment.'

The caller had her phone and Gill had mentioned the warehouse which meant the caller knew something!

'You said she's in bad way. How bad?'

'Bad enough. Better hurry!'

Those were the final words. Niven cursed as the phone went dead. Without hesitating, he shot off back into the traffic. Pedestrians turned their heads to stare at the crazy driver, outraged at his speed. They were just a blur of faces to Niven. When he came to a pedestrian crossing and was forced to stop, an old couple doddering across cost him precious time and tested his patience to the limit.

Short wasn't saying much, just rattling off directions. Niven's driving was terrifying him and his pained expression spoke for him. He'd read his boss's mood, decided discretion was the better part of valour and for once kept his counsel. When flashing blue lights appeared ahead, Short pointed, didn't need to elaborate on what those lights meant. Soon the car was speeding over the rough track to the dilapidated warehouse, towards the police car and ambulance sitting ominously outside the building. The scene was reminiscent of so many other tragedies the detectives had encountered that Niven's imagination went into overdrive. Sweat poured from his forehead, ran down his face. He could taste salt on his lips.

He parked the car, leapt out, took only a few steps before a swarm of yellow coated paramedics, emerging from the warehouse like busy bees from a hive, brought him up short. They were carrying a stretcher, fussing over whoever was on it as though they were transporting the queen bee herself. Caught between twin desires of wanting to know yet wanting to remain ignorant for fear of what he might discover, Niven couldn't move. Then Short pushed against him and propelled him forward.

'Keep back!' a yellow coat ordered as they joined the flow, craning their necks to see who was on the stretcher.

Niven barged through a gap, glimpsed a pale face, cheeks so white they almost matched the pillow. Red hair framed the face like a ring of fire on a bed of snow, confirming his fears and setting his heart thudding. Bile suffused from his gullet, erupted in his mouth. He'd seen dead bodies with a better pallor than Gill's. He leaned over the stretcher, called her name.

'Easy now!' a voice warned.

An arm gripped his, held him back. He dragged his eyes away from Gill's face, stared glassily at the paramedic who had hold of him, wrenched words from his own mouth.

'Is she—'

His voice trailed away, unable to pronounce the word 'dead' because, once he said it, it couldn't be recalled, would require an answer.

Short came up beside him, helped the paramedic restrain him until the stretcher disappeared inside the ambulance. The paramedic turned to him, his eyes reflecting a mixture of cautious wariness and compassion as they assessed the detective.

'She's alive, but she's gone into a coma. That's all we know for the moment, I'm afraid.'

Coma! That meant she wasn't dead. It meant hope!

That initial feeling of relief soon hit a plateau and he plummeted to the depths again. You could come out of a coma, he knew, but it could take time, years even. Even if you did recover, sometimes you were never the same person, lost something there in the darkness that was part of the real you.

It was all too much for him. As though he had just stepped off a fairground waltzer and the world was shifting under his feet, he staggered backwards. Then a second stretcher appeared, but he was only vaguely aware as it was lifted into the ambulance.

The noise made by the doors slamming jolted him out of it. As he watched the ambulance pull away, a cold anger supplanted his confusion.

Short, who had been watching solicitously, saw the change in him, placed a hand on his arm. Shrugging it off, Niven started towards the warehouse. The place looked so desolate it felt like the last staging post on the route to hell. Why on earth had Gill come here?

The uniform on the door recognized the detectives and waved them both in. DC Maggie Campbell was standing just inside talking to two uniformed constables. She knew Niven and Gill. When she saw him, she halted mid-conversation, stared at him sad eyed, floundering for words. Saving her the trouble, Niven made a gesture with his hand that told he already knew the worst.

Striding past them, he walked further into the building, to the edge of the illuminated circle, focused his attention on the body lying in the glare of the spotlights. Maggie and Short came to join him, keeping their counsel. Finally, he spoke to Maggie. 'Don't spare my feelings. Tell me what happened here?'

Maggie and Short exchanged glances. She pointed to the chains.

'The guy they've taken away was hanging up there and in a bad way. The corpse, as you can see, has a bullet in his brain.' She hesitated, swallowed hard. 'Gill was a few feet from where we're standing – unconscious – blood on the back of her head. There was a piece of scaffolding lying next to her.'

The silence that followed was broken by Short, 'Anyone identify the men, Maggie?'

One of the uniforms standing a few feet away, heard and chipped in, 'The corpse is Terry Brannigan's son, sir. I've had dealings with him.'

'I recognized Billy Paxton, aka Billy the Whizz, on the stretcher,' Short added.

'Yes,' Maggie confirmed. 'He was the one hanging. He'd been whipped.'

A soft, cooing sound came from overhead. Niven looked up, spotted two pigeons balancing on a beam and preening themselves. Had Gill, like those pigeons, been an innocent witness to this mayhem and paid for it? What was she doing in a dump like this in the first place? Those were the questions that he needed to answer.

'Any theories, Maggie?'

The DC drew a deep breath. 'Best guess, drug dealers falling out, turning against one another.' She looked down at her feet. 'No idea why Gill was here though.'

'Neither have I,' Niven said. 'But I do know the shooter rang emergency services to try to save Gill and, whoever he is, he knows us both.'

Surprised, Maggie stared at him with wide eyes.

'The shooter rang me, told me he'd called them,' he explained. Tears welled up in his eyes. 'Somehow he knew Gill and I – had – a relationship.'

Silence fell on the three detectives. Niven wiped his eyes. The shooter's voice replayed in his head. With that implied intimacy in his tone, the educated way he phrased his sentences, the coolness, it had been as though he was discussing an everyday occurrence, not the taking of another human life. The word psychopath came to mind. Was he someone Gill and he knew as a normal human being, never imagining what lurked beneath the surface? Gill's pallid face as she'd lain on the stretcher flashed into his mind. He fought the tears again, knew, if he didn't want to break down in front of the others, he had to get away, be on his own for a while.

'Think I'll head off to the hospital,' he announced, wearily.

'I'll come with you,' Short said.

Maggie's female intuition was at work and shook her head covertly and the DC got the message that he wouldn't be welcome.

'Unless Maggie needs help,' he added, hastily.

'She will,' Niven said and walked away.

Back in the car, he sat for a moment, fighting his emotions, guilt mainly. Gill had been alone in that awful place and he felt he should have been there to protect her. What on earth had she been doing in that den of iniquity to start with? Deep down, though it was more intuitive than logical, he had a creeping suspicion he was part of the answer to that question.

CHAPTER 19

He drove back to town on auto-pilot, joined a queue of traffic on Marton Road. Memories of driving the same road to see his father in hospital came back to him, made him feel worse than he already did. He parked in the north car-park, entered the hospital through the revolving doors and approached reception, steeling himself for the worst. The girl at the desk told him Gill was in intensive care and gave him directions.

The labyrinthine corridors were no longer quite such a mystery to him and he felt as though history were repeating itself: that it was only yesterday he had walked along them to see his father. He remembered that last visit too well, the long walk back to the exit, the sadness, the sense of aloneness starting to encroach on his soul, Gill pulling him round. Those emotions, followed by the violent confrontations the night he'd arrested Jack Cannon, could have acted as a catalyst he supposed, set him off wondering about all that business of who he really was, contributed to his doubts about continuing in the job. Or was he deluding himself? Perhaps it would only have been a matter of time before all that would have boiled to the surface anyway.

Intensive Care! The words illuminated above the entrance to the ward seemed too bold, too brash, a danger sign. Niven didn't allow himself any hesitation, walked straight in. Flashing his warrant card, he told the nurse at the desk he was a detective and a friend of Gill's, waited while she went off to find a doctor.

She brought back a young man with a tired, care-worn face who seemed too young to carry the burden of administering to those hovering in that twilight zone where one mistake could be the difference between life and death. His face was difficult to read and didn't give anything away as Niven introduced himself all over again. When the doctor started to speak, Niven concentrated hard, looking for signals that the words coming out of his mouth might mask the true prognosis for Gill in order to spare his feelings.

'The good news is that she came round for a few minutes,' the doctor said. 'However, she couldn't remember who she was or what had happened to her. Right now she's in a deep sleep.'

Niven didn't know what he should think or feel. It felt like a miracle she'd emerged from the coma so quickly. But if her memory was affected...?

'But she will remember,' he said, searching the doctor's face for clues, the burning intensity in his eyes willing the man to give an answer he wanted to hear. 'I mean – when she comes round again – she'll remember. It's temporary – isn't it.'

The face gave nothing away. 'We're hopeful. The good thing is she woke up. It's a matter of watching and waiting now.'

Niven looked down at his feet, taking comfort from what the doctor had told him, yet aware that he wouldn't be able to relax until Gill was back to her old self. He still couldn't shake that guilty feeling that what had happened to her was in some way connected to his own life. She'd walked into a criminal haunt which was as far from her normal milieu as you could get, but an integral part of his world. Why, for God's sake would a schoolteacher do that?

'A blow to the head sometimes causes amnesia,' the doctor explained. 'It's often temporary. We've given her a scan which only found a slight skull fracture, so there's a good chance she'll make a recovery.'

Niven brought his eyes up sharply. He didn't like those words 'often temporary'; it left room for too much doubt. But the doctor had shown optimism. That was something to cling to, to get him through for now at least.

In a sympathetic gesture, the doctor touched his arm. 'Do you know her family, her next of kin? We need to inform them.'

'Her father disappeared when she was a child and her mother died. She has no brothers or sisters. There's an aunt and cousins in Australia. That's all.'

'The aunt should know. Could you inform her for us?'

Niven nodded assent. 'Do you think I could look in on Gill?'

'We'll be doing more tests very soon, so it'll have to be only for a minute or two. But please don't disturb her in any way.'

The doctor sent for a nurse who led Niven down the corridor and off into a small room with only one bed. Gill was flat out surrounded by monitors and machines with tubes protruding and crawling over her body in complicated convolutions. He thought them grotesque, something from another world invading Gill's body with evil intent. They'd shaved off her glorious red hair and her face was small and fragile. Her hairless skull, reflecting the light, was like translucent ice, so brittle looking he thought it might crack if he touched it. Towards the back of the skull was an indentation, a miniature valley set in a purple and yellow landscape. His throat dried up. She looked so vulnerable he wanted to pick her up in his arms, drag her back to the warmth, make her remember. But he was powerless and he knew it, so he stood there, tears rolling down his cheeks, offering silent prayers, making promises to God he wasn't sure he could keep, if only He would bring her back.

Someone touched his arm and he turned to see a nurse beside him. She told him he'd have to leave, not to worry, they'd be taking the best care possible of the patient. He heard his own voice mumbling thanks. Then, he walked out onto the main corridor and slumped into a hard chair, his mind still with Gill in that prison of a room, fearing that even if she awoke again she might not know him, might remain in a perpetual limbo for the rest of her days....

Self-recrimination was not long in coming, followed by a sense of shame. He'd complained to Gill about his feelings of being rootless, an orphan again, without any consideration for her feelings, even when she'd reminded him her father had abandoned her and her mother while she was an infant. What had he been thinking? If only he could turn the clock back he'd have kept all that to himself.

The clink of cups and cutlery broke into his reverie. An auxiliary worker pushing a trolley of plated meals hurried past. With a heavy heart, he stood up, re-entered the ward, gave the duty nurse his card and asked to be informed if there were any changes in Gill's condition, for better or worse, then walked back onto the corridor again and headed for the exit.

Just as he was about to leave the building, he hesitated, remembered Billy Paxton had been brought to hospital too. If he was able to speak, perhaps he could throw some light on what had happened to Gill in that warehouse. He needed something to distract him, keep melancholy thoughts about Gill at a distance. Better to be doing something rather than brooding, wasn't it? Making his mind up, he turned on his heel, approached the main desk again, asked the receptionist where he'd find a patient by the name of Billy Paxton.

CHAPTER 20

A constable, whose ample stomach gained extra emphasis from the way he slumped in his chair, was on duty outside Billy Whizz's room. Following protocol, he was there for the criminal's protection but Niven thought that was like locking the stable door after the horse has bolted and anyway this character would probably take too long to struggle out of his chair in an emergency. Lost in a man's health magazine, he didn't even notice the detective approach.

When Niven spoke to identify himself, the constable wriggled around like a beached walrus and finally managed a more upright position. Niven considered reprimanding him for his slovenliness in a public place but let it go.

Billy was propped up on pillows, slim torso bound with bandages. His cheekbones were purple and swollen, eyes so deeply sunken they seemed to be hiding away from the world that had abused him. He was staring at a wall with a lugubrious expression, as though he was watching a drama being played out there that nobody else could see. Judging by that look, whatever he was seeing was making him miserable. Niven wondered whether he was reaching back, reviewing the parts of his life that had led him to this, wishing he'd done something differently.

Niven hauled a chair away from the wall, put it next to the bed. Billy heard the scraping sound, jerked his head around, then grimaced when he saw his visitor.

'Copper,' Billy rasped, voice so throaty it was a pretty good impersonation of a dalek. 'There's always one appears when you don't need him – or don't want him. Story of my life in'it.'

'From what I hear someone nearly wrote the last chapter of your life story, Billy, and it was no copper, my son.'

'Naw, man, it was all just for show. Wouldn't have gone that far.'

'Some show,' Niven snorted. 'Look at you, feller. He used a whip on you, I heard. No doubt there'll be scars. But worse than the scars there's the humiliation, the shame, if you catch my drift.'

Billy glowered at him. 'Don't know what you're on about.'

Niven manufactured a sigh. 'Me and my colleagues could put it around that you and Darren had a thing going, that you were into that sado-masochism stuff. That's how it looks with all those chains and the whipping. Get the picture, Billy son. Your mates would never look at you the same again. They'd be laughing behind your back, calling you a pervert.'

'You wouldn't do that.'

Niven gave a knowing smile.' 'Course we would. But it doesn't have to be like that, does it?' He leaned back, folded his arms. 'You're our only witness, Billy. You tell us exactly what happened in that warehouse and our lips are sealed. But it'll have to be the truth. We find you lied to us – well – your mates could die laughing and you'll have a permanent beetroot for a face.'

Billy was silent for a moment, staring at that blank wall again, his bottom lip protruding. The lips and swollen cheeks did nothing for his looks, just gave him a passing resemblance to a gargoyle. Niven figured he was running imaginary scenarios through his head, considering the embarrassment, the humiliation, if the threat was carried out. Eventually, he looked sideways at the detective.

'It'll just be between you and me. Nobody else will know I spoke.'

Niven shook his head. 'No need for it to go beyond this room.'

Billy faced him full on. 'It's my brother got me into this,' he whined. 'He's been shooting his mouth off to your lot, hasn't he? Hoping it'll get him a reduced sentence. Terry Brannigan got to know, got worried he'd grass on him. Darren lured me to that warehouse, tortured me, filmed it on his mobile and sent it to his father's phone.'

From the bitter resentment in Billy's tone, Niven was sure he was telling the truth.

'So Brannigan will use it as a warning to your brother. That it?'

Billy sighed. 'My brother's in with the VPs, but they've got phones in there. Terrry Brannigan will find a way to make sure he sees the video. Darren said if Don didn't take the warning I'd be a dead man.' He gave a hideous grin. 'But it's Darren who's dead, ain't it. The bastard got what he deserved!'

The grin quickly changed, his lips pulling back into a grimace to reveal a set of disgusting, yellow teeth.

'Terry Brannigan might think I had something to do with Darren's death and send people to get me. Talking to you is big risk, in'it.'

Niven was thinking about those phones. He'd heard of prisoners using them to run their drug empires from jail, one going as far as to contact his opposite number in a South American jail to arrange drug imports. What was the point in catching criminals for that to happen once they were incarcerated? It was demoralizing and one more example to make him question his career choice.

'Tell me about the woman, Billy,' he said, pushing those thoughts aside to concentrate on what he really wanted to know. 'Any idea what she was doing there?'

Billy cleared his throat. 'She just appeared out of nowhere, man. Darren put the lights on, chased her, hit her with a piece of scaffolding. Then this guy appeared with a gun. He made Darren tell him why I was being tortured, then shot him. I was half out of it. It was like a dream, a nightmare, man.'

'You'd never seen the woman before, or the shooter?'

Billy shook his head. 'Don't think so. State I was in, blood dripping into my eyes and that, I could just make out what was happening. I think the shooter had blonde hair. His accent was different, local but ... like ... posh, no slang, like he was educated or something, a snob – not one of us.'

Niven had little doubt that Billy was telling him the truth. He looked so pathetic lying there that, if he hadn't known he was a low-life, a drug dealer, responsible for bringing misery to so many users and their families, he might have felt sorry for him. As it was, he'd had to disguise his contempt for his lifestyle in order to get what he wanted. Being nice to those you despised was part of the job. You switched to another persona to communicate on their level. Perhaps the beating would make Billy think about changing his ways. Then again, perhaps Boro would sign Ronaldo from Real Madrid.

He rose, pushed his chair back against the wall. Billy had given him as much as he could and he had a picture now of what had gone on in that warehouse. But he still didn't know what Gill was doing there.

'Take a holiday,' he told Billy as he made for the door. 'Make yourself scarce for a while. Think about things. Next time you might not survive.'

As he drove away from the hospital, his only thoughts were for Gill. He wished he could have been there to protect her. She was a kind, good person and didn't deserve what had happened. Where was the justice in this world? Was life governed by an arbitrary fate working regardless of how you behaved? Strip all the sentimentality away and all the evidence seemed to point that way, didn't it? Nevertheless, hoping against hope there was a compassionate, divine being who had His reasons for everything, he said a prayer for Gill. What else was there to cling to?

CHAPTER 21

Back at headquarters he wandered into the incident room, studied the white board to see if there had been any developments; he sensed his colleagues watching and wondering about him. They would know by now what had happened to Gill and were trying to read his body language, afraid to ask in case it was bad news. Eventually Short approached, dragging his body across the room as though it was encased in a deep sea diving suit. He looked Niven in the eye, for once struggled to find words.

Niven spared him the effort. 'She woke up but she's got amnesia.'

The DC had the sense not to offer platitudes, but patted Niven on the shoulder in a show of silent empathy.

'She's got a good chance,' Niven said, 'but I don't want to think about it too much or I won't function. So it's best I just keep busy.'

Short nodded. 'Johnson asked to see you in his office the minute you came back in.'

'Thanks, better not keep him waiting, then.'

He ascended the stairs to Johnson's office on the next level, knocked and entered when the DI called out. Johnson was at his desk. He noticed his boss looked tired around the eyes. Long hours and too much paperwork were obviously taking their toll.

'How is she?' the DI asked, immediately pushing papers he'd been studying to one side.

Niven repeated what he had told Short. Johnson offered his

sympathy, asked him how he was feeling. Niven said he would cope if he was kept busy.

Johnson ruminated for a moment, then said, 'They've given me the warehouse murder. I could use you but I think it's too personal. Perhaps you should just stick to investigating Jimmy Peacock's murder.'

Niven, not liking that idea at all, lowered his eyebrows and thrust out his jaw.

'I can handle both, sir. Matter of fact I've already had words with Billy Paxton in the hospital and learned quite a bit.' He added, in a tone that left little room for doubt, 'With respect, sir, right now I need to keep very busy.'

Johnson sighed, but gave way, 'Fair enough. But remember you've got to stay impartial. It'll be hard to do that, but no personal vendettas because of Gill, eh! I need every man I can get, so if you can do that, it'll help. Now, sit down and tell me what you got out of Billy Whizz.'

Niven gave him Billy's version of events, told Johnson he didn't know why Gill was at the warehouse. He explained about the warning phone call from the killer, his reference to Gill as 'your woman' which meant somehow he knew them both.

'I can't think of anyone of our acquaintance, in or out of uniform, that it could be,' he added, stroking his chin thoughtfully. 'But there again murderers don't often stand out, don't go around with signs on their heads, do they, sir?'

Johnson frowned, pulled his bottom lip down as though he was trying to sculpt it into Mick Jagger's, then gave it up and spoke out.

'Well, it's a positive clue anyway. Keep excavating your memory. The link must be in there somewhere.' He paused thoughtfully, worked his tongue into all the corners of his mouth. 'It's possible he knew Gill, only knew of you, or the other way around. Think along those lines as well.'

'What about the video sent to the prison, sir? Shouldn't we do something about that?'

'Get onto prison security. Make sure they know we'll need the video as evidence – if they can find it.'

'Consider it done,' Niven said, adding. 'I presume the tech boys already have the bullet that killed Darren Brannigan. Any idea how long they'll take to analyse it?'

Johnson shook his head. 'How long is a piece of string? I'm still waiting on a report on the bullet that killed Peacock. I've asked for it as a priority, of course. Much good that does, eh!'

Niven understood how frustrating that must be for his boss. Forensics seemed to have a perpetual backlog these days, which seemed to indicate they were either short of staff, or crime was a growing industry. He figured probably both.

'Here's one outstanding thing,' Johnson continued, frowning enough to furrow his brow with deep lines. 'Our killer used a fire door near the roof to enter the building. There were fresh imprints in the dust on the stairs – from the same kind of boots issued to our uniforms.'

'Just like—'

Johnson cut in, finished it for him. 'Like the imprint in Peacock's flat, except these are a size smaller.'

Niven thought about that while Johnson worked at that bottom lip again.

'Same guy wearing different size boots,' Niven offered. 'Sometimes I wear a size bigger. Nothing unusual in that.'

'If he's a copper, it would fit in well with the idea that he knows you and Gill, wouldn't it?'

'So we're back with our killer cop – or two killer cops.'

Johnson leaned back. 'We need to know about those bullets. The bullets will tell a tale. If the same gun fired both, it's near on certain it's the same killer.'

Niven started to say something, hesitated, then said it. 'The killer claimed he saved Gill's life, then rang emergency services. Could it be this killing wasn't planned, just evolved … to save Gill? Is that too far-fetched?'

'It's possible, but why did he want to know the reason Billy was being tortured? He obviously wasn't there at the start of proceedings. You're sure Billy didn't mention the killer was wearing a police uniform?'

'His vision was clouded with his blood and he couldn't see detail.'

Johnson did a drum roll on the desk with his fingers. 'There was no calling card like there was for Peacock so maybe we're building sandcastles.' He drew in a breath, let it out in a long, meaningful sigh. 'We need those damn bullets analysed – like yesterday. Otherwise we're turning circles.'

For a moment the DI seemed lost in a mist, his mind, oblivious to his surroundings, tunneling for a glimpse of light. Niven had to manufacture a cough to remind him he was still there.

'Sorry,' Johnson said, blinking his way back. 'You go off now. Don't forget to ring the prison. Type up your report about Billy Paxton for the office manager then scoot off home and get some rest. You've a testing time ahead. What with Gill and work demands you'll need plenty of rest.' He softened his tone. 'And don't bottle anything up. Talk to me if you feel the need.'

Niven headed for the door, grateful he had a boss in Johnson who had retained the human touch even when he was under strain himself. He'd never seen the DI lose it except when it was justified and he considered him a good role model. Would he be able to retain his own equanimity under the same pressure, he wondered, or, under real duress, would he revert again to that devil who'd been a fraction away from beating Jack Cannon's brains out? The thought made him fearful.

As soon as Niven left the office, DI Johnson reached for the phone. His hand hovered for a moment, then, racked by indecision, he withdrew it. He knew he'd made a promise to his old friend to keep him informed, but this was serious stuff and he wasn't quite sure how he'd react. Where deep emotion was concerned, you just never knew with people, sometimes even with those you'd been close to. One mistake, one rush of blood to the head and his friend might ruin himself by interfering where he shouldn't. You couldn't play with people's lives.

But loyalty meant something to Johnson, which was why he reached out again. Again, his hand hovered. Again he didn't pick up the phone. Maybe it was better to let this ride for a while. After all, he could keep an eye on his sergeant, gauge his reactions at fairly close hand without doing him any favours. If things got worse, maybe then he'd inform his friend, though, in truth, even then he wasn't sure it would be the right thing. He had a loyalty to his sergeant too.

Back in his own office, Niven got on the phone to Clem Davis, the Security Chief at Stockton Prison. They'd had previous dealings and so he knew him quite well. He told him about the video and its intended purpose. Clem wasn't surprised; mobile phones were the latest bane of his life. He said the prisoners were locked up for the night but, as it happened, officers had been detailed to carry out routine searches on Brannigan's wing the following morning. He'd include Brannigan's pad amongst those targeted so as not to arouse suspicions that they were onto him. If they found anything, he'd let Niven know.

The detective thanked him, finished the call and got down to typing up his report. An hour later he'd finished, handed his report to the office manager, gave those colleagues working late a perfunctory wave and headed off home.

He was glad to get back to his flat with its view over Hartlepool marina. He took stick from Middlesbrough colleagues for living there, had learned to smile indulgently when they called him monkey hanger, an allusion to the citizenry of the town who once strung up a monkey thinking it was a French spy. It was worth the grief though, because he'd always wanted a place overlooking water and boats and this was the nearest to that ideal he could find near his work. Usually, the view helped him to relax.

On the way home he'd bought fish and chips. He sat in a chair at the window to eat them straight from the paper, helping them down with a can of coke. The wind was gathering force now and the boats in the marina danced to its tune. But he knew the wind was merely flirting, skirmishing for the storm brewing out there on the horizon where he could see brooding clouds gathered in a council of war. The groaning wind and the depressing gloom in the sky did nothing to cheer him, it seemed merely to emphasize that all was not right in his world; it enhanced a sense of loneliness in a universe too great for a mere human to begin to comprehend.

He thought about Gill lying there in the hospital, the good times they'd shared and he wished now he'd appreciated her more. You never knew what you had until you lost it. He knew now how true that was. But he hadn't just lost her, had he? Of his own volition, he'd pushed her away.

He picked up the phone, rang the ward, asked how she was faring, was told 'no change', two little words, but so very potent, so latent with possibilities, words which left him in limbo. Putting the phone down, he stared at the horizon with a heavy heart, until the travails of the day closed in on him and he slept where he sat, oblivious to the wind calling on its full battalions, the rain beating in a frenzy against his window, the boats enduring.

CHAPTER 22

While Niven lost himself in slumber in Hartlepool, a few miles away in Middlesbrough PC49 gazed around his flat, realized how much he'd neglected it, that it needed tidying, a good run over with a duster and a hoover. He'd always been fastidious about keeping it clean, but these days he found he couldn't be bothered. Like so many other things in his life, it didn't seem to matter any more. Even having to leave his job hadn't bothered him in the end. What had come to matter most was his project. Avenging his father was something he should have had the bottle to do years ago. It had taken a big shock to make him realize that and to transform himself from what he had been.

When the first low rumblings of thunder rolled across the sky, he rose and went to the window. He watched silver whips of lightning chastising earth and sky. Primitive man, in his ignorance, thought thunder and lightning an expression of their gods' displeasure. Had he been any less ignorant in his own beliefs, he wondered? He wandered to the bookcase, plucked the Bible from a shelf, flipped through the pages, soon dropped it on the floor with an exasperated sigh. 'An eye for an eye' or 'Thou shalt not kill' What was a mere man to make of such contradictions? He'd lived by the Bible until his trouble started, had tried to find comfort in it. But all he'd believed had fallen away from him, shed like a snake's skin once real problems came into his life.

He allowed there was still a possibility he was wrong – Thomas the Doubter! Part of him longed for that to be so. If there was an after-life and he met his father there, he'd explain the dilemma; punish the evil ones now or rely on hope that there was another life where they would suffer. Spin a coin! Throw the dice! Take your choice!

Jimmy Peacock, Terry Brannigan, Don Paxton. That had been the order he'd intended for his killing spree, the last named to die in the prison visiting-room, his final act of vengeance. But the detective's woman wandering into the warehouse, for whatever stupid reason, had gone and ruined it. The best laid plans of mice and men. Robbie Burns had been on the ball there. Well, he'd been a mouse most of his life. Now he felt much more of a man. Pro-active. No longer passive. PC 49 incarnate!

Improvize when a plan goes wrong. That was the key to success. With Billy Whizz in hospital, the idea of using him to insinuate himself into Don Paxton's life was dead in the water. There was the added risk, one he'd previously taken into consideration as worth taking, that, if Brannigan was caught intimidating Paxton, he'd have time added to his sentence. If that happened, how could he kill two men behind the prison walls? The clock on the mantelpiece ticked in the silence, seeming to mock him, reminding him that his own time for this was limited, that he couldn't afford to wait.

He sat for another hour, picking at the problem while the wind and rain lashed the window as though they bore a personal grudge. How could you kill two men in separate locations within a prison? His police uniform wouldn't even get him past the entrance, though a prison officer's uniform might.

Think again! Security would be well and truly prepared for that one and, even if he got past the gate, the problems would be as imponderable and unpredictable as the warren of corridors he'd have to pass through. Other ideas were dismissed as equally useless until, frustrated, he closed his eyes.

At midnight, he woke with a start, an idea in his head. Once, he might have called it divine inspiration. Now he considered it a gift from his subconscious mind, which must have been hard at work even as he slept. Set a thief to catch a thief. That summed it up neatly. Tweak it a little and you got set a gangster to kill a gangster.

Revivified, he levered himself out of his chair, opened the bureau drawer, removed the note book where he'd written down the phone number taken from Darren's mobile before he'd disposed of it. That done, he put on a raincoat and cap and walked out into the storm.

Within ten minutes, he was sitting in his car at a lonely spot beside the River Tees, the phone in his hand. He thought about sending a text, decided against it. He wanted to hear a voice. Only that way could he be sure he'd provoked the right reaction. Hearing Brannigan suffer would be an added bonus.

Staring out across the dark river, he rehearsed the words and tone he would use to gain maximum effect. Then, when he thought he had it right, he dialled the number.

The answering voice was sleepy, irritated, 'Yeah, Darren. What is it?'

'That's Terry, I presume!'

In the silence that followed PC was sure he could feel menace emanating from the gangster even down the phone.

Eventually, a rough voice said, 'Don't presume with me whoever you are. Where's Darren? Put him on now!'

'Darren's – indisposed.'

He heard a long, drawn breath and smiled. He wanted his man agitated.

'What's going on? Is this a joke?'

Brannigan was making an effort to restrain his anger, but PC could hear it in his voice. To fan the flames of that anger, he laughed down the phone.

'No joke! When I said indisposed that was just a euphemism.'

'A what?'

PC adopted the scholarly, long suffering tones of an academic of a certain type who thinks anybody who doesn't understand his subject is a fool and lesser mortal.

'A euphemism, for your elucidation, is the substitution of a milder expression for a stronger one, when the stronger would be more accurate.'

That led to another silence, then, 'Put Darren on, you faggot.'

'Darren's dead! That's not a euphemism. It's plain fact.'

PC waited, relishing the moment. This was no more than the man who'd ruined his father deserved.

Brannigan laughed, but it was a nervous laugh. 'Darren's high, out of his head, ain't he? He's put you up to this. Thinks he's being funny.'

'Not a man used to listening, are you, Terry? Believe me, your son's dead as a doughnut and I'm the man Don Paxton hired to do it. He was way ahead of you, Don. He thought you might suspect him of grassing, asked me to watch over Billy, kill anyone who tried to harm him. All your fault of course.' PC sighed theatrically. 'Don told me to say you always underestimated him. You're next to go down, by the way.'

Brannigan, in a frenzy, fired a volley of curses down the phone, outlined graphically all manner of things he was going to do to his caller. PC waited. When the list was exhausted, all he could hear was heavy breathing of a man with a fury in him that had nowhere left to go.

'You're a bastard liar! You ain't killed Darren!' Brannigan continued in a last flurry. 'Paxton ain't got the bottle. This is some kind of wind up. You'll pay, whoever you are!'

Quite calm, PC answered him. 'Ring his girlfriend, or his mother if she's stupid enough to be around still. The police will have informed the nearest and dearest by now, I would think. Likely they'll be telling you in the morning, if not in the next hour or so.'

Before Brannigan could respond, smirking his satisfaction at the way it had gone, PC cut him off, stepped out of the car. He walked to the river bank and hurled the phone into the water then stood for a moment, enjoying the feel of the wind and rain against his cheeks, the sound of the water lapping up time. At that moment, even though he knew it was a delusion, he felt so alive and free.

CHAPTER 23

Brannigan didn't waste any time. He didn't like Darren's live-in girlfriend, considered her an air-head blonde, beneath his son. She was the only bone of contention between them. But this was a case of needs must, so he rang the house.

Part of him felt foolish doing it, the part that wanted to believe the call was a hoax; he figured someone with a grudge against him had stolen Darren's mobile – was winding him up. Yet he couldn't deny he was afraid. There had been something about that voice, a detached coolness, as though its owner was beyond fear and it held no power over him. In fact, he'd seemed to relish laughing in its face – in his face.

As soon as she heard his voice, the girlfriend burst into tears. He immediately feared the worst, fought the urge to yell down the phone at the silly cow, tell her to pull herself together. Finally, she calmed down, told him the police had informed her Darren had been shot dead in the warehouse.

His world tilted, everything slipping and sliding. The girl babbled on, but it was inconsequential; her words didn't reach him. Sweat poured from his forehead and trickled down his back. He shut her off mid-flow, stood in the middle of the cell, shoulders hunched, hands over his face, the weight of his grief like a malevolent force pressing down on him.

In a daze, he slumped onto the bed. Nothing seemed real, everything around him blurred, as though the world was an alien place, part of another dimension he was merely observing through frosted glass. Darren dead! Never in his wildest dreams would he have imagined his only son would go before him. Dead! Such a short word to have such potency. Applied to his own son, it grew to gigantic proportions, eclipsed everything, changed everything.

Just when he could taste his freedom, his world had come crashing down. Darren, the only family he had, the only person in his life he could trust one hundred percent, had gone and left him. He'd been thinking of all those things they'd do together once he was out. Now all his plans and dreams had been ruined. He'd be going out to nothing, nobody that mattered. A tremor ran through his body like an electric shock. Suddenly the winter of old age didn't seem so far away.

He peered through the bars, glowered at the mocking moon, its rotund face as bright and merry as a buttercup while the light that sustained him was diminished to a mere flicker. Dark clouds, as though complicit with his mood, converged to smother the moon and the cell became dark. Now another face sprang into his mind. He could see Paxton sneering, comfortable in the knowledge there were prison walls between them. Grief turned to anger, anger at the man he'd thought he'd known and hadn't really known at all; he felt anger at the miscalculation that had cost him his son's life. Well, Paxton would find out there was nowhere to hide. Even if it took him the rest of his life, he'd make sure he paid the price.

Born of grief and fury, the idea came to him in the deep of night, Jack Cannon at its heart! He could use his cousin's recent incarceration as a means of extracting retribution. Jack was with the VPs rather than the mainstream because he owed too many people money. It was better to live with the paedophiles and nonces than to end up with a knife in your gut because, even if you could take care of yourself, there would always be a moment you dropped your guard and someone, either for money or to make a reputation with the big boys, would stick you.

The point was Jack would be in daily contact with Don

Paxton. Brannigan had sent him money in Spain, but that wasn't the main reason he could call on him. Jack was a little crazy in the head but as sound as a pound where family were concerned. He'd been fond of Darren, even had him over to Spain a couple of times when he was hiding there. Brannigan had taken the way Darren died as a personal insult. Jack was like that, plus a little unhinged and crazy enough to do anything.

His hand shook as he rang his contact on the VP wing, gave him the story and asked him to tell Jack he'd appreciate it if he could deal with Paxton for him because he couldn't do it himself. If he needed help, he knew one of the screws – a man who'd been photographed in a compromising situation with a prostitute – who would assist him. The screw did duty on the wing on Thursdays and would provide Jack with a weapon, or a door left open, whatever he considered necessary.

When he finished the call he sat down on the bed, brooded over the fact he wouldn't be there to savour the moment when Paxton got his come-uppance. He hoped his cousin wouldn't make it too quick, too painless, for the bastard.

He suddenly realized the phone in his hand was compromised now. Whoever it was had called him earlier could easily inform the prison he had a mobile in his cell. Best to get rid of it rather than risk time being added to his sentence and the sooner he did it the better.

Slackening the stitching on his duvet, he reached inside the material, extracted a length of cord. Then he went to the window, put his mouth against the bars and called out to his neighbour. Eventually a sleepy voice answered from the adjacent cell.

'It's bloody late,Terry. I was in Honolulu enjoying myself, mate. Bit of a shock to wake up in Her Majesty's waste disposal unit.'

Brannigan wasn't in the mood to exchange banter.

'Got a phone I want you to hide.'

'What's wrong with it?'

'There's a chance they might get onto it, come searching my cell.'

'You're playing pass the parcel bomb with me!'

'What's up with you,' Brannigan snapped, in no mood for an argument especially as this guy owed him big time for favours rendered, and this was a small favour, virtually risk-free. 'You can get rid of the phone – as soon as. How's that a big problem?'

'OK! OK!' the voice came back at him, its tone more amenable now, but without any enthusiasm.

Brannigan ejected the sim card, slipped it into a cavity in the toe cap of his trainer, placed the phone inside a Nescafe coffee tin. After that, he secured the lid and tied one end of the length of cord around the tin like a sling.

'Get ready!' he hissed through the window.

Holding the tin, he extended his arm through the bars as far as it could go, then let the tin go so it was hanging on the cord which he swung back and forth like a pendulum, gradually building up momentum. From previous experience, he knew how much force would do it and eventually his neighbour's hand grabbed the tin. He waited a few seconds while the phone was removed, then, given the word, reeled the empty tin back in.

After his exertions he lay down on the bed and closed his eyes, but he couldn't close out the memories that came flooding in: Darren as a child: Darren as a boy growing into a man. He cursed himself for not being there to protect him and came as near to feeling guilt as he ever had in his life. Jail, he'd always considered an occupational hazard that you just endured until you got out again and resumed your old lifestyle; he was used to jail. But now the cycle had been broken. He wouldn't be able just to pick up where he'd left off. He groaned knowing this was going to be the longest night of his life, a foretaste of so many nights to come without the comfort of his son on the outside. Would he ever get used to that? They said time was a healer, didn't they, but he had his doubts.

CHAPTER 24

Niven had risen early, hurried his breakfast so that he could beat that cursed Marton Road traffic and visit the James Cook Hospital briefly before he turned in at work. Right now he was concentrating on the doctor's face, fearful he'd be hearing that phrase 'no change' again in response to his inquiry. But the news was heartening today because Gill had awoken knowing her name, address and that she worked as a teacher.

'She'll make a full recovery, then,' he said, making it more statement than question, as though his optimism could compel the doc to agree.

A shaft of sunlight from a skylight lanced down onto the doctor's head and shoulders. He blinked, stepped back into the shade, the glare too strong.

'Suffice to say it's looking hopeful. But we're not forcing her. That could be counter-productive.'

Niven hoped the doc was being extra cautious and felt he couldn't afford to let him think all was well even if there was the slightest chance of a setback.

'Is it possible to see her?'

The doctor nodded. 'For a few minutes. But whatever you do, don't press her if there are things she's struggling to remember. We're in a delicate situation here and we want her to take her time.'

'Understood,' Niven said. 'I won't.'

He walked into the ward feeling light headed, as though he'd been drinking and reached that state when everything takes on a rosy glow. After a bad night full of dark imaginings, it seemed the new day was beginning well. Gill had come round and knew who she was. His prayers were being answered. Last night, each flash of lightning, each roll of thunder had brought with it terrible visions of her lying forever in a hospital bed like a vegetable.

He deflated a little when he saw her because nothing seemed to have changed since his last visit. She was still hooked up to all those tubes, her face was still ghostly white and her eyes were shut. He sat down beside the bed appreciating the doctor's caution. Then, suddenly, as though she'd sensed someone there, her eyes fluttered open.

His smile came involuntarily, born of relief and love for the pale face looking up at him. But, like the last rays of the evening sun dipping below the horizon, day conceding to night, his smile gradually slipped away. Gill was staring right through him as though he was made of glass. If, as they said, eyes were the mirror of the soul, her soul seemed absent. At best, all he could detect in those eyes was neutrality and he was certain she didn't know him. His hopes plummeted back to the depths from which they'd risen only moments ago.

'It's me, Gill,' he said. 'It's John.'

The eyes blinked, but showed no recognition. It was as though the Gill he knew was lost in that mythological place where lost souls wait, not knowing who they are or what they seek. If it had been a physical barrier between them, he would have ripped it apart with his bare hands. But how could you fight what you couldn't see?

'Pleased to meet you.'

Her voice took him by surprise. He hadn't expected it. It was a small consolation, though, because she really didn't have a clue who he was. She was merely being polite – the way she would be to a complete stranger and that felt like a dagger to his heart.

Tears came, but he fought them back. The only person in the

world who really knew him, knew his hopes, his fears, his inner thoughts, didn't recognize him any more than she would someone who'd wandered in off the street. He knew it was selfish, but those feelings of being alone, an orphan in the world, that had threatened to overwhelm him when his father died, returned. He felt drained. All he thought he had once been seemed a delusion.

Gill's expression had changed again. She was gazing at him almost in wonder now, as a baby might stare at something or someone seen for the first time. It was better than that coldness, but still devastating.

'Do you work here?'

He felt an irrational impulse to take her by the shoulders, shake her until she remembered who he was, what they had meant to each other. But he would never do that and he remembered the doc telling him he hadn't to press her because it could set her back.

A lump rising in his throat, he spoke gently. 'That's right. I work here. We're looking after you. Please don't worry about anything.'

With that, he rose from the chair. He wanted to stay with her, but knew it wasn't a good idea because he was unnerved, not in control of his emotions. Forcing a smile, he gave her a little wave and made for the door. Once he was outside the room, he leaned on the wall, closed his eyes, cursed his weakness.

The doctor was nearby, in deep conversation with a nurse. He broke off as soon as he spotted the detective, came over, asked how it had gone and whether he was all right.

'She didn't know me,' Niven mumbled. 'I should have expected that, I know, but it was quite a shock. I had to get out of there.'

The doctor nodded, his sage eyes studying the detective.

'That's the way it is with these things, I'm afraid. Some memories return, other areas remain blank. But it's still early days and the fact there's been progress is a very good sign.'

Niven swallowed hard. 'She will remember me – eventually?'

'No guarantees, but I'd say there's a fair chance.'

'Is there anything I can do to help her?' he said. 'Something that might help her remember?'

'Keep visiting. Next time just talk about anything that you did together and above all be patient. In the meantime you could go to her home, bring things which are very personal to Gill, items of clothing, perfumes, photographs, those kind of things. Sometimes they can trigger memories, start the ball rolling.'

'Yes,' Niven said, seeing the sense, a little embarrassed by how he'd reacted. 'I have a key. I could do that – thanks.'

The doctor touched his arm, guided him towards the exit.

'You've had a bit of a shock, you know. Best you keep yourself busy and not brood. Rest assured we'll be doing everything we possibly can. As I say, she has a fair chance.'

Niven shook the doc's hand and walked out, back into the corridors where, preoccupied, he lost his way for the first time since those early visits and had to retrace his steps to find the exit. What kind of labyrinth was Gill's mind wandering in, he asked himself. Would she be able to find her way to the exit, find her life again, find him? He worried what the doc might not be saying, from kindness, was that she might never come back to him again. You never know what you have until you lose it. What kind of fool had he'd been to let her go in the first place? He prayed to God she'd recover, have a normal life, with or without him.

CHAPTER 25

Gill's cottage was in the pretty village of Thorpe Thewles, on the outskirts of Teesside. She called the cottage a haven, a place where she could retreat from the world, enjoy the countryside, the changing colours which came with the seasons. It replenished her spirit, she said, gave her fresh impetus when she returned to the urban jungle. Niven, too, found his own sense of peace when he came here because it was so different from the concrete jungle where he operated. There, another side of nature, red in tooth and claw, snarled in your face and you couldn't drop your guard because complacency could cost you everything.

Today, though, as he reached under the loose stone where Gill kept a spare key, he didn't feel much at peace. That he could feel Gill's presence the moment he walked up the garden path didn't help. A spasm of guilt disturbed him as he unlocked the door because he was intruding into her private world while she lay helpless. Trying to shake it off, he stepped into the kitchen, found a plastic bag in one of the cupboards and went to work searching for things that might stimulate her memory.

At first, he selected antique ornaments and a mug which had her name printed on it. Then, he realized his conscience was restraining him, that she had belongings and items which were much more personal. Trying to ignore the feeling he was snooping in areas of her life he shouldn't, he proceeded from room to room, looking through drawers, collecting perfumes, CD's, pieces of jewellery, photograph albums, piling them in a desultory fashion on the living-room sofa.

When he'd finished, he slumped down, picked up a photograph album, idly flicked through it. Many of the photographs were of Gill and him together. But there was one of his dad and him just before his dad fell ill, arms around each other's shoulders. He turned it over, saw Gill had written, 'I love these two' on the back. The words went right to his heart.

Telling himself he'd indulged his emotions enough for one day and to get on with the task in hand, he selected a few photographs he considered would mean more than the others. One of them was of Gill and her fellow students at university on the day they'd collected their teaching degrees, all smiling, bright eyed and bushy tailed, as though the world could never touch them, that they would always remain as they were that day.

As his eyes scanned the faces, they stopped at the individual on the end of the back row. There was something familiar about him, but he didn't know why. He'd met all Gill's friends and he was pretty sure he wasn't one of them so that couldn't be it. More likely he was someone he'd seen around the town, or come across briefly in the course of his work, one of those faces he'd registered vaguely but had no particular reason to file away for future reference.

Just as he was about to give up, his memory rewarded him. The hair was a touch lighter and longer, the face leaner, less careworn, but he was sure it was the teacher who was in trouble for beating a pupil, the one whose interview he'd sat in on at the last minute. He remembered, though he'd felt sympathy for him, he'd found him a little weird.

He figured it must be just pure coincidence that Gill and he had graduated together. Given the group was large, around fifty students, the chances were Gill and he were no more than acquaintances at most. Gill had once told him she hardly mixed outside her circle of friends who took sciences, so she had probably hardly known him. Dismissing the matter as inconsequential, he made a final selection, piled everything into the bag hoping there'd be something to kick start her memories.

Placing the bag near the back door, he stood motionless for a moment, in his mind's eye seeing Gill scurrying about the kitchen that day she'd moved in, smiling, happy she was coming to live in the country. Her mood had drawn him in like a moth to a bright light.

He forced himself back into professional mode. Somewhere in the cottage there might be a clue to the reason she'd gone to that warehouse. He shouldn't leave without looking, should he? One last inspection, this time with his policeman's head on rather than as a friend couldn't do any harm and might yield something.

A second exploration yielded nothing but frustration. Then, as he was about to call it a day, he remembered the telephone. He supposed he should check for messages on the answer machine. He wandered into the hall, picked the phone off it's cradle, aware this was yet another intrusion into Gill's personal life.

A metallic sounding voice announced she had seven messages and he trawled though them. The first four were from female friends, all of whom he knew. They didn't provide him with any clues. Two of them commiserated with Gill, mentioning him, telling her not to worry it would all work out. That just made him feel bad.

The fifth message really got his attention. He didn't recognize the female voice, but from its timbre he guessed it belonged to a much older woman. The content intrigued him enough to play the message again.

'I'm Mary,' the voice began, the tone nervous as though the speaker wasn't sure of herself. 'I got your letter. Everything in it was correct. It was a shock – you can imagine – but I've hoped for something like it all these years. I'm frightened and thrilled at the same time. I'd like to meet as you suggested. Could you make Prior's café in town, say on Friday around 2pm. If I don't hear from you, I'll assume that'll be OK. Oh, and I'll wear a yellow scarf so you'll know me.' A deep, sigh of relief, then, 'And thanks my dear. It means so much. You've no idea.'

Niven played the message a second time. The quiver in the woman's voice, her emotional state, the fact that so much seemed unsaid, intrigued him. Whatever Gill had written was obviously of momentous import, for her anyway. But what could she have written to a woman she didn't know that could cause such heightened emotion? It was a mystery, but there was no indication it had lured Gill to that warehouse.

The woman had proposed meeting Gill at Prior's Café on Friday at 2pm. Today was Friday and it was approaching midday. Judging from her mood on the phone, she was going to be very disappointed when Gill failed to turn up. He supposed the least he could do for Gill, who hated letting anyone down, was to pop along to the café and let the woman know what had happened. At the same time, he could investigate whether the matter between them could possibly be connected with the business at the warehouse, though in truth he had little hope that would be the case. Before he left, he played the remaining messages but they were just from colleagues of hers and of no consequence at all.

CHAPTER 26

Back at headquarters, as soon as he entered the incident room, he sensed a change in atmosphere, thought he could detect a renewed sense of purpose amongst his colleagues, wondered what had brought it about. Returning to his own office and assailed by sudden hunger pangs, he searched his desk for a chocolate bar, found one he'd left there, had just taken his first bite when Short knocked and walked in.

'Bad diet, sir!' Short said, pointing at the chocolate. 'You'll end up a chocaholic like DI Johnson.'

Niven took another bite, smacked his lips defiantly. 'What doesn't kill you makes you stronger and I need strength.'

Short sat down, folded his arms. 'Came to tell you we've got the report on those bullets. Apparently the same gun killed Peacock and Brannigan. The brass are really worried now it could be one of our own turned serial killer. They want us working flat out. The DI's showing the stress. He's on his second choc bar.'

Niven swallowed the last piece of the chocolate. He couldn't say he was surprised it was the same gun for both killings. What puzzled him was why, if it was the same killer, he'd shot Darren Brannigan to save Gill, and called the emergency services for her. Equally puzzling, the guy had known he and Gill were close. What kind of mind was at work? What was the connection he couldn't find?

'Our man left a calling card at Peacock's flat,' he mused. 'Serial killers supposedly stick to the same *modus operandi*, don't they, so why didn't he leave us something at the warehouse?'

Short shrugged his ignorance, softened his voice and changed the subject.

'Have you been to see Gill?'

Niven nodded. 'She's improved. She's remembering things.' His gaze drifted away from the DC to a blank wall. 'But she doesn't remember me.'

When he turned his gaze back to him, Short dropped his eyes and looked down at his size tens.

'I'm sure it'll all come back to her, sir,' he mumbled, adding. 'Can't understand what it was she was doing in that warehouse in the first place, though, can you?'

Niven rubbed chocolate from his mouth, cleaned his hands with tissue.

'I'm doing my best to find out, speaking of which – I've got to slip away soon. If the boss asks, tell him I searched Gill's cottage and I'm following a minor lead.'

'You'll be OK, won't you? I mean – it's all a bit close to home.'

'Rather be working on it than tearing my hair out wondering. Thanks for your concern though.'

The DC took the hint, stood up and made for the door.

'Just so long as you know you can count on me if there's anything you need.'

'Yeah! I know I can. Thanks.'

Niven killed an hour on paperwork, but time dragged and he found his concentration wavering. It was a relief to finally slip on his jacket and leave the office.

Walking to the car, he tried to bring back the killer's voice. It had been muffled, but that of an educated man, he was nearly sure. No matter how he searched his memory, he couldn't place it in another context. How had he known about Gill's and his relationship? Why had he saved Gill? Those questions kept nagging like toothache because, if only he could find the answer, their man would be served up to him on a plate.

As he drove into the Cleveland Centre in the heart of Middlesbrough the dark clouds which been hovering gave up their burden, with all the pent up fury of a besieging army unleashed on the enemy. Rain hurled itself against the pavements, ricocheted off them like miniature silver spears. Niven didn't think he'd seen the sun for a few days and wondered if it had gone into mourning. Wipers on full speed, he swung into a car-park, collected a ticket, parked and, jacket hauled over his head, sprinted for Prior Café.

CHAPTER 27

It was not your average meat and potato establishment. Round tables with carved legs peeping from beneath starched tablecloths, delicate chandeliers hanging from the ceiling, gave it an ambience that seemed suited to a clientele of old ladies fond of afternoon tea and scones washed down with the latest gossip. Most of the tables were occupied, mainly by the middle-aged or older.

Suit damp from the rain, Niven stood inside the doorway, ran a hand through his hair, cast his eye over venerable heads, looked for a woman wearing a yellow scarf and spotted her at a corner table. At first glance, he figured she was in her mid-forties, give or take a couple of years. She was dressed smartly, hair neatly coiffured and impressed him as a woman who took pride in her appearance, but knew enough not to go for overkill. He noticed she was sitting upright, rather stiffly, like a worried mother in a hospital waiting-room, unable to relax until she knew everything would be OK for her child. He supposed her discomfiture fitted with the idea of a woman who said she'd been waiting for years for whatever Gill had to tell her. Unfortunately, he was the one who was going to have to disappoint her.

As he wove his way through the tables, she arched her back, moved her head to the side, trying to look around him towards the door. But he was blocking her view and she was forced to focus on him as he halted a foot away from her table. A querulous look from her made him feel like a naughty child, so he decided he'd get straight to the point.

'I'm afraid Gill's not coming.'

Her eyes seemed to leap out of their sockets at him and her lower lip gave a small quiver. A pained look, something close to agony, came into her face as she stared, shoulders falling forward as though her whole body was deflating.

Niven shuffled his feet. Seeing her reaction, he regretted now he hadn't approached the matter more subtly. He could see meeting Gill had meant even more than her message had intimated. What surprised him was the swell of sympathy he felt for her as he stood there not quite knowing what to say next. A drop of rain running off his collar and tracing its way down his backbone like a cold finger stirred him into action.

'May I sit for a moment and explain?'

She looked up at him vaguely, her mind clearly somewhere else. Then, her surroundings seemed to register with her again. She gave a little shudder.

'Please – do.'

He sat down, offered her his hand across the table. 'I'm John Niven, an old friend of Gill's. I'm afraid she's had an accident … been … hurt.'

As they shook hands, the woman's eyebrows knitted into a frown.

'Hurt! What happened? How bad is she?'

Niven didn't want to go into detail, not when there was no need, so he decided to give her the bare bones, enough to explain Gill's absence.

'She received a blow on the head and she's lost some of her memory. It's early days, but the doctor is hoping it'll come back – sooner rather than later.'

'The poor girl!' the woman said, adding with an air of wistfulness, 'This was to be our first meeting. I don't really know her but – how did you—?'

'I listened to her messages on the answer phone. That's how

I knew she was to meet you here today.' He softened his voice. 'I could tell this meeting was very important to you, so I decided Gill would want you to know why she couldn't be here.'

'It was very important,' she said, weary resignation in her voice. 'I do hope she'll recover. That's the first priority, of course it is. We can always re-arrange. Kind of you to come, John. I'd have sat here all afternoon – hoping.'

Niven shook his head. He'd given this woman a shock and he knew it.

'I do have an ulterior motive as well.'

She looked him straight in the eye, puzzled. 'Ulterior motive?'

'Don't worry, I am a friend of Gill's, but I'm also a policeman. It was no accident Gill was hurt. Your message had an air of mystery about it, left me wondering whether you would know whether Gill was in any kind of danger. We have to follow up everything, you understand. For that reason, I'd be grateful if you could tell me the purpose of your meeting today.'

The woman's cheeks flushed. Her fingers clenched into fists. You would have thought he'd asked her to betray a secret she was guarding with her life. Could that be simply to do with the fact he was a policeman, Niven wondered? Some people reacted to policemen like that and he supposed his manner had been a touch more formal than he'd intended.

She gradually unclenched her fingers and placed her hands flat on the table. He could see she was steadying her nerves. Twice she opened her mouth to speak. Twice nothing emerged. Finally, she bent her head, clasped her hands together in an attitude of prayer and spoke in a small voice.

'I'd rather not tell you if you don't mind. It's difficult because another person is involved. I wouldn't want to hurt this person and our business can have nothing to do with Gill being injured I can assure you.'

She unclasped her hands jerkily, as she did so knocked the milk jug over. Full of nerves, she grabbed a napkin, dabbed at the spilled liquid. Niven felt himself growing suspicious and spoke out in a forthright manner.

'I have to tell you this is part of a murder case, so I'd prefer if you let me be the judge of whether it's relevant or not. Everything you tell me will be in strictest confidence. Don't forget Gill is a friend.'

She stared at him with an intensity that burned. He'd seen enigmatic faces in paintings, faces that seems to transcend time and place, faces that embed themselves in your subconscious as alluring mysteries. Niven couldn't fathom why, but in that moment, for him, hers was such a face and he felt a little unnerved by her.

'Gill and I don't know each other. She wrote to me, that's all.'

'Yes, you're wearing the yellow scarf so she'd recognize you. That's how I knew you. But that doesn't answer my question.'

An aroma of freshly made coffee drifted by. Like a distant battle, a clash of steel cutlery emerged from the kitchen. Niven saw in her eyes that she was fighting her own inner battle, this woman he barely knew. His best guess was this was all to do with Gill's work as a teacher, an emotional matter, perhaps concerning a pupil whom, as she was inclined to do, Gill had gone out on a limb to help. This woman could perhaps be a close relative or—

Finally, with a long sigh, she composed herself and gave him an answer.

'Gill found something out about my past, wrote me a letter, a very kind letter. She wanted me to confirm – what she'd found out – stressed she wouldn't do anything about it, that it wasn't her place to interfere in my private life.'

Niven mulled that over. Looking at this gentle, rather refined woman, he found it difficult to believe that, whatever was haunting her, it could have any bearing on what had happened to Gill. But, having come this far, he wanted this matter out of the way.

'This secret. Best you tell me straight out. Then we can both forget I know – providing it has no bearing on what happened to Gill.'

She placed her elbows on the table, covered her face with her hands, stared at him through the bars formed by her fingers. Finally, she slid her hands away and emerged from behind those bars to meet his gaze.

'You've every right to ask,' she said. 'Of course you have. It's foolish of me to think otherwise.'

Niven leaned towards her. 'Please understand it gives me no pleasure to press you, but in murder cases everything has to be considered.'

Silently nodding, she stared at a far corner of the room.

'I suppose it's a commonplace occurrence, a story as old as time,' she began. 'It's just when it happens to you, it's so shaming. You see, I had an illegitimate child when I was a very young girl. My parents made me have the poor mite adopted, then moved the family away. It was to give me a new start they said, as though I could just dismiss the child and the father like that.' A tear dropped from her eye, making a small damp spot on the tablecloth. 'Something like that never goes away. It stays with you forever. You always wonder.'

Her story resonated strongly with the story of his own birth, he had a strange presentiment he knew what was coming next. Thinking he was being ridiculous, he tried to shuffle the feeling off.

'Gill had been doing some research,' the woman continued. 'She knows the child – my son – and believes he needs to know his natural parents. She wanted to know how I felt about that, suggested we could meet to discuss the matter.'

Niven's body tensed. He couldn't drag his eyes away from the woman's face. Those words, 'She knows my son!' reverberated in his brain while the question he knew he had to ask next flashed into his brain. He opened his mouth, but the words he needed wouldn't reach his lips and died in his throat. The woman was staring at him now, her face betraying she knew something had disturbed him. Dropping his eyes, he rose from the table, the clumsiness of his movements rattling the cutlery and crockery.

'Excuse me,' he stammered, moving away from the table. 'Call of nature.'

Niven was grateful the toilet was unoccupied. He needed a moment alone to compose himself. Standing at the sink, he splashed copious amounts of water onto his face, the cold liquid refreshing him, but doing nothing for his disturbed state of mind. He told himself to get a grip but kept coming back to the fact Gill had gone to a great deal of trouble to find the woman and he was nearly certain, knowing his background, she'd done so as a favour for him. Yet, there was more to it than that and he knew it. Right from the moment he'd first looked into her face, he'd felt a connection with the woman that he hadn't been able to fathom.

The door opened and an old man shuffled in, disturbing his reveries. As he headed for the urinal he hesitated, stared at Niven, his face and eyes wrinkling in kindly concern.

'You OK, son?' he asked. 'You look like you've seen a ghost.'

Niven forced a smile. 'Maybe I have,' he said. 'Not sure.'

The man frowned, moved on. 'Don't worry about it,' he called over his shoulder. 'I've seen ghosts and it's the living that bother me, son.'

Niven stared at his face in the mirror. Those features looking back at him had been shaped by generations of ghosts he would never know, each one leaving an indelible imprint. Out there in the café there could be one of them and he had to face up to it, ask the question. But how did you say to someone 'I think I'm your son' without them thinking you were mad. And what if he was wrong? How foolish would he feel then? Yet, he realized he was just postponing the inevitable, that it had to be done, so he ran his comb through his hair, smoothed down his jacket, breathed in deeply and stepped back into the café.

CHAPTER 28

Heading back to the table, he felt a strange excitement coursing through him and his stomach muscles were knotted as tight as the day he'd sat his police entry exams. He was aware of her eyes following his progress across the room. As he pulled the chair out and sat down again, he could see bemusement behind her smile, knew she'd noticed he was acting strangely. Had she any idea why, he wondered.

'Sorry,' he muttered.

'When you gotta go, you gotta go,' she said, maintaining the smile. 'Nature's an unstoppable force, isn't it?'

'There's no denying it,' he said and, not wanting to delay any longer in case his courage failed him, got on with business.

'This son? Did Gill tell you his name, anything at all about him?'

She shook her head. 'That's the reason we were meeting. She was going to tell me about him, learn a bit about me. Then, if my son was agreeable, she was going to introduce us.'

Niven voice came out as a hoarse whisper. 'Your name, it's Mary Sawyer, isn't it?'

She stared at him in amazement, then narrowed her eyes, a question looming there. Niven saw she was bursting to ask, but struggling.

She gave it up in the end, just nodded affirmation and with that simple action he knew this woman was his mother, that Gill had found his mother for him.

'I think – I'm – your son,' he stuttered, the bald statement seeming too simple, too stark for the weight it carried. 'I'm adopted. My mother's name was Mary Sawyer. She lived in Grove Hill, Bank Road.'

Tears glistened in her eyes, slid down her cheeks. She reached out, took his hand, her eyes fixed on his face as though she feared if she looked away, even blinked, he might disappear, give the lie to the moment.

'I was born in Bank Road,' she said, struggling to keep her composure. 'I felt something when I saw you, but I knew I was in a state coming here today, susceptible to my imaginings, you see, so I dismissed it.' She wiped tears away with the back of her free hand, but her eyes still didn't leave his face. 'You don't know what this means to me.'

He gripped her hand tighter. Those times in the past when he'd imagined meeting his mother like this, he'd thought he'd be cool, feel little for someone he didn't know. He'd read about such meetings in books and magazines, that sometimes it was just like two strangers meeting to exchange pleasantries, drifting apart afterwards. But this wasn't like that at all: it had taken him completely by surprise because in his bones he could feel a powerful connection with her.

He became aware of people at the surrounding tables staring. She sensed it too, withdrew her hand from his, fumbled in her bag for a handkerchief, dried her tears and made an effort to compose herself. He noticed the little shake in her hands.

'I called you Thomas,' she said, smiling. 'But now you're John.' She caught the throb in her throat. 'I'm so sorry, John, so sorry.'

'No need to be,' he muttered. 'I had good parents – none better, a good life, sometimes I've wondered about you though. Who you were, what you were doing?'

'Thank God you didn't suffer,' she said, 'I worried in case you ended up somewhere horrible. I had nightmares about it – prayed for you every night.'

'Well, the nightmares can stop now. I was fine.'

They talked for the next hour, catching up on each other's lives, gaining the confidence to ask more intimate questions. Mary explained she'd been just sixteen when he'd been born, going with a boy a little older. Finding herself pregnant had been devastating, it had brought her to the edge of a nervous breakdown. Her parents had taken over and she'd just gone along with their wishes, like a sheep, she said with obvious anger at herself even after the passage of the years. Later, she'd married a good man but been widowed young. There'd been a daughter to that marriage so he had a half-sister ten years younger than himself. When Gill had contacted her, it had been like a miracle, one she'd prayed so long for.

'Gill's made it possible,' she said, 'but it wasn't at your instigation, was it? So why did she do it?'

Niven shook his head. 'After I'd lost both parents, I started to feel like an orphan. In spite of the fact I had been loved and nurtured, I felt something was missing. It started to affect me and my relationship with Gill. She must have decided to do something about it.'

'I'm glad she did.'

He didn't like to tell his mother that his insecurity had caused a split between them.

'So am I. Gill probably knows what's good for me better than I do myself.'

'From her letter, she sounds a nice person, considerate of other people.'

'That's her and now she's in trouble.'

He suddenly realized the happiness he'd felt meeting his mother had led him to lose track of time and purpose. He still had to get Gill's personal effects to the hospital and his colleagues were working flat out. This meeting had been a wonderful interlude, but the world was calling him back.

'This has been fantastic,' he said, understating it, 'but I have to visit the hospital and I'm supposed to be trying to solve a murder. The strange thing is the killer has some unknown connection with Gill or me, maybe both of us.'

'You said one reason you came here today was that you thought I might be able to help you?'

He smiled. 'Looks like that turned out to be a dead end.'

She reciprocated his smile, then a shadow of concern fell across her face.

'This won't be a dead end for us, will it? We can meet again, can't we? You've a half sister I want you to meet. To lose you again after—'

His mother's obvious concern touched him and he was quick to reassure her.

'Nothing would please me more. But right now needs must. I'm afraid I really have got to go.'

She ferreted in her handbag for a pen and paper, scribbled down her address and telephone number, pressed it into his hand. In turn, he gave her his card and she leaned across the table to kiss his cheek, her show of affection catching him by surprise.

'There's one thing I was sure you would ask,' she said, as he rose.

Niven thought he had a pretty good idea what she meant.

'If you're talking about my birth father, I just thought you'd get around to telling me who he was in your own time – if you wanted to.'

'That was kind, but it's no problem. I'm sure you'd like to know and as it happens Gill mentioned in her letter she thought she'd found him. You would like to know, wouldn't you?'

'Of course. But can a man get lucky twice in one day? Meeting you has been amazing.'

She beamed at the compliment. 'Well, your father lived in Grove Hill as well. I haven't seen or heard of him since before you were born. His name is Terrence Brannigan.'

A spasm like an electric shock coursed through Niven's body.

All the strength seemed to leave his legs so that he had to reach out and lean on the chair to steady himself. He didn't know how he managed it but for his mother's sake he maintained the outward illusion that he was unfazed while his insides churned.

As far as he was aware, there was only one Terry Brannigan in Grove Hill. He was about the right age. Surely his mother couldn't know what kind of man he was or his name wouldn't have tripped so easily off her tongue – not without her burning with shame. Then, it came to him what Gill had been doing in the warehouse. Not realizing Brannigan was in jail, she must have gone there to speak with him and couldn't have chosen a worse time to do it.

'Thanks,' he mumbled, masking his feelings. 'Perhaps we can discuss him another time. Got to fly now – really.'

With a little wave, he left her, made for the door and stepped outside. He stood there for a moment, sucking the fresh air into his lungs, trying to come to terms with what he had just heard. It had been wonderful to meet his mother, but the weight of her last piece of news had crushed him. With a heavy tread, he made his way back to the car-park, oblivious to the rain, Terry Brannigan's name repeating in his head like a curse descending down the years.

CHAPTER 29

The incident room was so busy nobody paid Niven too much attention. He was happy about that because, preoccupied with other thoughts, he didn't feel like talking. Once he was in his own office, he closed the blinds, shut out the world and slumped in his chair. He felt like a boxer who'd gone ten rounds in the ring and, just when he thought the fight was won, had been punched to the canvas in the last round and was struggling to get back onto his feet.

His mother had been so warm, so elegant. Meeting her had been like living a beautiful dream. But it had been devastating to hear his father was a particularly nasty criminal. Had that temper of his, the one he thought he'd mastered until it returned with a vengeance the night he fought Cannon, come from criminal genes: nature laughing at nurture? He caught his own reflection in the monitor on his desk, studied his face. Features could be inherited, why not a nasty nature? He hoped to God whatever was lurking beneath his features favoured his mother rather than Brannigan.

The big question was what was he going to do next. He realized he should go to Johnson, inform him Gill had gone to the warehouse looking for Brannigan, thinking she was finding his father for him without knowing he was a gangster currently domiciled in Stockton Prison. He was reluctant to do it because he knew these things had a way of getting out and eventually it would become common knowledge. For the rest of his life, he'd have to endure sly glances and innuendos.

The computer was sitting right in front of him. Leaning forward, he tapped into the Police National records and typed in Terrence Brannigan's name, started to read his record. His father's criminal credentials stood comparison with some of the worst he'd come across. That it fell short of murder seemed to have been a matter of luck combined with an ability to hide his tracks. He'd been a murder suspect on a few occasions, but though the circumstantial evidence was as good as it got, solid proof was missing.

As Niven delved deeper, he found the names Paxton and Peacock recurring. Especially in their younger days, they had been Brannigan's main partners in crime. Robbery with violence seemed to have been the trio's speciality.

He sat back, chewed on a nail, pondered the links between those names. The killer had eliminated Peacock, then almost certainly Brannigan's son who'd been torturing Billy Whizz at his father's bidding in order scare Don Paxton. But what had the killer been doing in the warehouse in the first place? He seemed to have come out of nowhere to save Gill and hadn't hesitated to kill Darren.

He hadn't acted like a paid professional in any way so it wasn't too far fetched to speculate he'd killed Peacock because of a personal grudge. Could the grudge extend to the other two members of the terrible trio? If that theory held water, Paxton and Brannigan would be on his list. But they were incarcerated, impossible for him to get at. Niven's frustration built by the minute. If only he could find a link between the killer and those three men?

He went back to the computer, this time concentrated on the times the three recidivists had worked together, reading through each case twice. Something dragged his eyes back to a report on a post-office robbery sixteen years ago. As the three men were escaping, they'd walked right into a bobby on foot patrol and beaten him badly. They'd been caught and done time for that one.

At first, he couldn't figure what had drawn him back, but when he studied the photo of the policeman's bruised face and the name, PC Thompson, he knew what it was. Thompson, he recalled, was the name of the teacher he'd helped interview, the one who'd suggested there was a certain empathy between them. The same character had appeared in Gill's graduation photograph. The detective recalled Thompson had seen Gill in the foyer at HQ on the day of his arrest. Billy Whizz described the killer as having sandy hair and an educated voice; this teacher had sandy hair; his voice was cultured. But what really got Niven's juices going was the strong resemblance of the man in the photo to the teacher.

He told himself to slow down, get a grip. Coincidences happened. Likely he was reading too much into something that would prove to be nothing? Yet he knew he couldn't let go until he'd satisfied his curiosity and the only way to do that would be to go back and look at PC Thompson's record, find out a bit more about him. Given the passage of time, more than likely they'd be in a file in a dingy basement, gathering dust. Well, he'd just have to visit the Records Department. Experience had taught him face to face contact was always better than a phone call if you wanted to speed things up.

Relieved he had a task to help him stop brooding about his criminal father, Niven headed into the Incident Room. He intended to slide out in the same manner he'd entered and use the lift to descend to the basement of the building where old paper files were kept. DC Short was over by the window engaged in conversation with an attractive female constable, he was seemingly so engrossed that Niven thought he was going to make it out without being seen. He was wrong. Just as he reached the door, the DC called across the room.

'Did you get anywhere, sir?'

Niven sighed. A maelstrom was brewing up inside his head, with the result right now he felt about as communicative as a monk under a vow of silence and didn't want to talk to anybody. But he considered Short a good lad at heart and he didn't want him to feel he was deliberately cutting him out of the loop, so he made the effort and crossed the room to where the pair were standing. But once he reached them, he just stood like an idiot struggling for anything meaningful to say. Short, aware something was wrong, stared at him.

'I mean, sir,' the DC stuttered, glancing at the policewoman. 'Last time we talked you were going to follow up a clue you found in Gill's cottage, I think you thought it might lead somewhere....'

Niven wasn't prepared to tell anyone what he'd learned about his family connections, not yet anyway – if ever, in fact. Neither was he ready to voice suspicions about the Thompson business until he had something more definite. Feeling increasingly foolish, he tried to think of something to break the uncomfortable silence that was developing, but words seemed to have deserted him. He saw that Short and the woman were starting to look embarrassed now, so he forced a grin and made an ill judged attempt at levity.

'Didn't get anywhere,' he muttered and transferred his gaze to the woman. 'Poor chat up technique like my DC here, I suppose.'

As soon as he'd said it he realized how crass it sounded and wished he could call it back. Short was more sensitive than his occasional brashness suggested, and he was blushing now. The woman didn't look too pleased either, judging by the way her eyebrows rose in silent reprimand. Niven knew he'd never have said it normally and tried to retrieve lost ground.

'Sorry. That was a stupid remark. Put it down to the fact I'm tired.' He patted Short on the back, transferred his gaze to the woman. 'He's a sincere bloke this one, and professional about his work.'

Neither replied. Short, puzzled by his boss's uncharacteristic behaviour, just looked down at the floor. Niven, afraid if he said more on those lines he'd dig a deeper hole, changed the subject, tried to sound less of a neanderthal.

'Actually, I've been looking at a case from 1994. It concerns a uniformed policeman beaten up on patrol. Don't suppose either of you know anybody with a memory that stretches that far back who might be able to help?'

He'd asked the question to fill in a space, for the sake of something to say rather than with any expectation of a positive answer. But the woman came up with one.

'My dad has just retired after twenty-five year's service. He was uniform, working in the town mostly, and he's got a good memory. I'd put money on his knowing something about your man.' She glanced at the clock on the wall. 'Usually he's down the Viking at this time for a pint. He'd welcome a bit of a natter about the old days. Just make sure you've an excuse to get away or he'll turn it into a long session.'

Niven weighed it up. Personal recollections could often get you to the heart of a matter better than a bunch of records which, though they gave the facts, left much unsaid. What you were seeking wasn't always committed to paper, might lie in the character of a person, or something unrecorded, or perhaps obscured by a mass of detail. On the other hand, a visit to the pub might waste time better spent on the records, as tedious a prospect as that was for him. Seeing his hesitation, she waved her phone in the air.

'I'll give him a ring first, just to make sure he's there. If you give me a name I'll ask my father if he knows the person and you can decide whether it's worth the trip.'

She'd dialled before he had a chance to say anything and her father answered on the first ring. A short exchange confirmed he was indeed in the Viking and, after explaining why she was ringing, she asked Niven for the name of the policeman concerned.

Niven glanced at Short. He didn't think the name could mean anything to him, so there wouldn't be any harm done revealing it, but he felt uncomfortable because the DC would gather there was something he wasn't sharing. Yet, he knew he had to go ahead alone on this one.

'Ask your dad if he remembers a uniform called Thompson who was hurt back in '94 while apprehending villains raiding a post-office.'

She spoke again to her father, listened to his answer, told him a detective might call at the pub to have a word, then finished the call.

'He says he can remember the man and the incident,' she told Niven. 'If you decide to go see him, ask at the bar for John Walker.'

Envying her the easy, affectionate way she'd spoken to her father, he thanked her for her trouble. One glance at Short, who gave him a quizzical look, told him the DC knew something was going on and was still puzzling over it.

'Don't worry, it'll all come out in the wash,' he told the DC.

CHAPTER 30

Brannigan lay awake all night grieving over his son, hating the way that smooth voice had announced his death, as though his son was nothing but a piece of rubbish he'd disposed of. Besides his sorrow, there was frustration, because he wouldn't be able to do for Don Paxton himself, would have to settle for second-hand satisfaction when all he wanted was to put his hands around the rat's neck, look into his traitorous eyes as he slowly squeezed the life out of him.

When he was out of there, one way or another, no matter how long it took, he'd find Darren's killer and make him pay. That voice wouldn't sound so smooth and superior when it was pleading for mercy, begging for a swift exit from a world of pain.

A dull, insipid light seeped through the bars, painting everything grey. Brannigan heard the clink of keys echoing in the corridor. Dragging himself from the bed, he made an effort to compose himself. The day had dawned like any other day, but with Darren dead he didn't want to rise and look it in the eye, just wanted to lie down forever. Yet old instincts died hard. He wasn't going to let the screws see that he was in pain and so, when the door opened and one of them stepped in, he made his face as blank as the grey walls.

'Governor Platt wants to see you,' the officer announced in a perfunctory tone which, coupled with the lugubrious expression on his face, suggested the prospect of his day's work was seriously underwhelming.

Brannigan scowled, 'Governor Platt! You mean I've got to face him on an empty stomach?'

The screw raised an eyebrow. 'He calls, you come. Not going to have bother, are we? Not with your release date so close.'

The screw knew the score, exactly which button to press to ensure his co-operation. Equally, Brannigan knew if he was too agreeable the screw would have sensed something wrong with him.

Two screws were leaning on the landing rail no more than a few feet away from his door. As they passed, Brannigan caught the look that passed between them and the escorting officer, the latter's knowing wink. Did the fools think he was born yesterday? There was only one reason they were on the landing so early – a pad search. No prizes for guessing whose pad. But why this morning? Had the smooth voiced assassin tipped off the prison that he had a mobile phone? Well, if that was the case, he was ahead of the game. Even at his lowest ebb, grief crushing him, he'd anticipated the danger.

Governor Platt kept him waiting an age outside his office. Brannigan figured the the screws needed time to search his cell and Platt was giving it to them. Then, at last, two officers marched him in and stood at either side. The governor, sitting behind his desk, gave the prisoner an appraising look. Brannigan guessed he must have been around the thirty mark. Everything about him was pristine, from his smart suit and perfectly ironed shirt to his short, neatly combed hair. But the prisoner considered him just a boy dressed in man's clothes. What could he know about life at the sharp end? In a man's world, in his world, respect was earned the hard way, with fists and guts, not sitting in a fancy office pushing a pen around like it was a magic wand. He knew why he was here today, didn't want to hear it from the those soft, feminine lips.

'I'm afraid I've got bad news for you, Terry.'

The face was grave, the tone concerned. On stage, it might have passed as decent acting, but to Brannigan it was a travesty.

The governor allowed himself a dramatic pause while Brannigan waited, face impassive, playing along, letting Platt have his moment. He knew what was coming and while presenting an impression of calm fought to control himself.

'Something gone wrong with my probation, sir?'

Calling this boy-god, 'sir' left a bad taste but sometimes, just sometimes, you had to pay lip service.

The governor shook his head. 'I'm afraid it's worse than that, Terry.'

His melancholy tone would have been way over the top in a melodrama. Who did Platt think he was kidding? He didn't care a jot about Darren? Brannigan stared hard into his eyes, willing him to get on with it so he could get out of there before he puked.

'I'm sorry to have to inform you that your son Darren has been murdered.'

Laid out starkly in those formal tones by that little creep sitting behind his desk with all his straight-backed pomposity, it was another thrust of the dagger into his bleeding heart. Even though he'd heard it officially now, part of him still couldn't accept it; he imagined he'd suddenly awake to find it was a nightmare. He was aware of the governor's scrutiny and, not wanting to give him the satisfaction of seeing him in pain, he didn't alter his expression, responded with one word.

'How?'

Platt leaned forward, shoulders hunching, his body language implying he was about to impart confidential information, a favour he thought would please. Brannigan saw right through him and felt like stuffing his condescension down his throat.

'I've been informed he was shot in your,' Platt cocked an eyebrow, 'business premises?'

This time Brannigan allowed himself two words.

'That it?'

The governor's body unfolded. Sitting back, he eyed the prisoner. Brannigan was thankful he'd had the foreknowledge, otherwise there'd have been no telling what he might have done at that moment. As it was, he was struggling to hold back. Staring at a spot on the wall above Platt's head, making his words a matter of pure fact more than a question, he spoke up.

'I'll be going to the funeral!'

He brought his eyes back to the governor's face and using them as weapons, fired all his pent up fury at the governor.

'Yes, all being well,' Platt grunted, withering a little under the defiant stare. 'You'll have to be handcuffed, of course. We'll let you know the precise arrangements in due course.'

Brannigan tilted his chin. 'Yes – everything will be done in due course – sir.'

He hadn't been able to help himself, the hint of threat, the menace in his tone. Disconcerted, not sure how to react to it, the governor shuffled on his chair like a hen laying an egg.

'I can go now, can I – sir?'

Platt brought his hands together, fingers interlocking like the jaws of a trap.

'There is another matter of grave concern we have to explore.'

Brannigan looked at him hard.

'You did say "grave concern",' he said, putting unmistakable emphasis on the word grave. 'My Darren dead and you're making with the jokes, sir?'

It took a moment to dawn on Platt what he meant.

'I assure you that was not my intention,' he muttered.

'Well, then – sir – this matter? Is it "grave" to you or to me? Can't think of anything that could top what you've just told me, can you?'

Clearly displeased by the prisoner's surly tone and disrespectful manner, Platt puffed out his cheeks like a spoiled child in a sulk.

'Grave for both of us!' he shot back with a flash of temper. 'We've had reports you're in possession of a mobile phone, that it's being used to create serious trouble in my establishment. As we speak, my officers are searching your cell. Should they find the said article, it would not bode well for you or your chances of an early release.'

Brannigan could tell he was well under Platt's skin. The governor was showing his true colours now, firing off warnings at him while his son lay dead in a cold mortuary. One time that would have been enough inducement for him to leap over that desk and teach him a lesson, but age and experience had taught him that that would only bring him more trouble.

'Better you should tell us if you have a phone in your possession,' Platt continued even as he realized he wasn't getting any response. 'It would go better for you in the long run.'

Brannigan didn't want to look at the hypocritical creep any longer. Instead, he looked out of the office window, concentrated his attention on the building that held the vulnerable prisoners. Somewhere in that austere building Jack Cannon would be busy planning Paxton's demise. His cousin didn't mess about; it wouldn't take him long to put a plan into action. Preoccupied with that thought, he ignored the governor.

'Well, you've had your chance. I'll take your silence as a denial,' Platt said pointing his pen at him. 'Let's hope for your sake we've been misinformed.'

'Yes, sir. You'll let me know about the funeral, sir?'

Platt shook his head in irritation.

'Yes!'

'Very kind of you ... sir.'

As though a bad odour had assaulted his nostrils, the governor wrinkled his nose. He nodded at the screws standing beside Brannigan.

'Take him out.'

The same screw who brought him escorted him back, not a word passing between them. On the way, they met the officers who had been loitering with intent outside Brannigan's cell. They passed by in silence but the prisoner noticed one of them gave a slight shake of his head, read it as meaning they'd been disappointed as he'd known they would be.

Back in his cell, he stood by the window, gripped the bars and fixed his eyes on the hills. They triggered a memory, words he'd once heard from a vicar trying to convert him during his first spell in jail. 'I will lift mine eyes unto the hills – from whence cometh my strength and understanding.' It hadn't made sense to him then, still didn't. He was looking at those hills right now but garnering no strength from them. As for understanding, that was rubbish. No way could looking at hills make him understand why his beloved son had to die so young.

One thing he did understand, though, was the power of the fury inside him, what it could do, the strength it could give him. He'd managed to suppress it in the governor's office but he could feel its pressure growing, knew he couldn't confine it much longer. Eventually, when it became unbearable, he pounded at the wall with his fists until red rivulets ran from the peaks of his knuckles like the streams pouring off those distant hills which, like life itself, had lost their former allure.

CHAPTER 31

It was only a stretch to the Viking from headquarters. Niven walked it, hoping John Walker's memory would be in good working order when he got there because there was no time to waste. He had a hunch it wouldn't be long before there was another death.

The bitter sweet memory of the meeting with his mother was still fresh in his mind and his father's deathbed words, 'Let sleeping dogs lie,' repeated over and over in his mind. He recalled showing Gill his birth certificate the night they'd split up, was sure she must have seen his mother's name, leading her on the path to disaster. Well, now he certainly knew where he came from and it was a miserable thought.

Around tea-time he stepped into the Viking. It was only a quarter full, no doubt because those with families had headed straight home from work. The remaining clientele were groups of boisterous young men and women, chatter merchants letting off steam after the constrictions of the working day. Older, lone individuals, sat on the fringes, exiles from the mainstream. One or two of those were observing the younger elements as though wondering what all the noise was about.

He ordered a blackcurrant and lemonade, which the barman served him with a wry look. When he asked for Johnny Walker and made a joke about meaning in the flesh, not the hard stuff, the barman didn't even crack a smile as he pointed to a stout fellow sitting in a corner seat with a pensive expression, his head in a newspaper and a pencil in his hand. Niven made his way over.

When he was a yard away, Walker sensed his presence and looked up. Niven noticed the bright curiosity in his eyes, too bright for a man retired, he thought. But what did he know? He was already having doubts about the job at his age. Before he could introduce himself, the old copper winked and tapped the newspaper with his pencil.

'Three down, six letters. Another word for old bronze money?'

'Couldn't be "copper", could it?' Niven said, grinning. 'Here's me thinking I still have that certain air of mystery and you're on to me quick as a flash.'

Walker laughed and shook his hand. Niven momentarily glimpsed the daughter's face superimposed on the father's. Who said ghosts didn't walk the earth? They were right there in the gene pool. In the end there was no escaping them. Didn't he know it, too?

'My daughter's phone call was a bit of a clue but, truly, I saw copper written all over you as soon as you came in.'

'Really! Now I know why Lynx never works for me like it does for the lads in those adverts, the one the angels give up their halos for. It's not my deodorant makes me a social pariah after all.'

'No fallen angels in your life, then?'

Niven grinned. 'Only the fallen, never the angels.'

John Walker laughed in a 'been there done that way' which seemed to establish an implicit understanding between them. Then, he grew more serious.

'Believe me there are worse things in life than being a copper, son. Like being nothing at all, a nobody.' He stared across the room. 'Sometimes retirement can make you feel that way. Never thought the job possessed me to that extent, but now I know. Not good! Not good at all to let something take too much of you.' He gave a little shrug. 'But you don't want to hear about that. Sit down and ask away about your man.'

Niven parked himself on the seat, hoping this meeting would provide a breakthrough.

'Your daughter told you I was interested in a PC Thompson, who worked in the town back in 1994.'

'Yes, there was the feller hurt in a post office raid in Nunthorpe. I remember it well. As it turned out, he was hardly a good advert for the force, but at the time he had a lot of praise. As they do, the papers went overboard, called him a hero and the brass milked the publicity – as they do.'

Niven's spirits rose. This was the kind of knowledge he probably would never have gleaned from the records. He'd made the right decision coming to see this old copper.

'You're not exactly convinced he acted heroically?'

Walker leaned forward. His eyes seemed even brighter, as though he imagined he was back on the job again and relishing it.

'I had it on good authority he was visiting his mistress in the shop next to the post office, bold as you like too, in full uniform. He came out whistling, walked straight into the villains, he couldn't get out of their way and took a bad beating.'

That was exactly the kind of thing Niven was looking for, an insight into Thompson's character. John Walker was the garrulous type. If there was more, he felt sure he wouldn't have to push for it.

'So Thompson was a manufactured hero, like the character in that Dustin Hoffman film, "The Accidental Hero" I think it was called.'

'Yeah! Seen that one. Thompson milked the attention in a nauseating way. When he didn't get the rapid promotion he seemed to think was his right, he claimed he was getting headaches from a blow he took to the head.'

'Let me guess – he tried for compensation.'

Walker grinned wryly. 'Yup, but it backfired, like it always does when a man gets too greedy.'

'Backfired?'

'One doc who examined him was a sharp cookie. He couldn't find anything wrong with his head, but something made him suspicious. He did tests and found traces of cocaine. That was the extent of the man's arrogance, going for a medical with that stuff inside him.'

Niven gave a low whistle.

'Strewth! That would finish his career. Be lucky not to get jail?'

'What I heard, they investigated him on the quiet, found he was turning a blind eye to the activities of certain street dealers in return for supplying him. They never actually caught him selling drugs though.'

'Did they put him in prison?'

Walker shook his head. 'Shamefully, it was all hushed up. Police hero turns to drugs wouldn't have made good headlines. What I heard, Thompson made the excuse he was only taking the drug because of the terrible pain he was suffering from injury sustained during the assault. That suited the brass. It gave them a way out and he was told to resign or face charges.'

'So he resigned, did he?'

'Of course. No choice, had he?'

Walker supped his pint, licked the froth from his lips.

Niven waited, sensing the old policeman had more to tell, but would do it in his own time and that he was enjoying it as much as his beer.

'A thing like that,' he said eventually, staring into his glass like a seer seeking answers to life's mystery in the patterns formed there, 'always leaves a legacy – a stain on the soul that's hard to erase.'

Niven leaned forward eagerly. He had a presentiment that whatever was coming next would be the crux of the matter. Walker didn't disappoint him.

'A year after he resigned he hung himself, leaving a widow and children.'

Niven hadn't expected anything quite as dramatic. He took a moment to digest it.

'He hung himself because of what happened when he was on the force?'

Walker shook his head. 'Nobody knew the reason. There was no note. Who can say exactly what tips a man over the edge? That could have been part of it. Maybe a combination of things did it.'

Niven's mind raced with possibilities. Thompson's children would be adults now. If one of them believed the gangsters were responsible for their father taking his own life that could be a motive for exacting revenge. But all this happened back in 1994. Why wait nearly twenty years?

Raucous laughter from a group of youngsters disturbed his thoughts and he realized he'd been so preoccupied with what he'd just heard, he'd lost all sense of time and place. John Walker was staring at him quizzically.

'Enjoy your dream, son? Meet any of those fallen angels on the dark side, or just ghosts from the past?'

Niven eyed him sheepishly 'Sorry – just exploring for a moment.'

'Well, I can see what I've told you started a bush-fire anyway.'

Niven lifted an eyebrow. 'The widow and the kids. I'd like to know more about them. How many children were there?'

'Can't help you, but I have contacts, people who knew Thompson and gave me all the inside stuff at the time.'

Niven reached inside his jacket, slid his card over the table.

'Be grateful for anything. Wish I could tell you what this is about but it's based on hunches, might turn out to be a wild-goose chase.'

Walker wafted a hand. 'Don't worry about it. I had my time, son.' The old copper sighed. 'Only trouble is my daughter's following in my footsteps. Must be in the blood, I guess.'

Those damn genes again! They kept coming up like a plague

to remind him of Brannigan. Niven dismissed the thought, decided he could trust the old policeman enough to throw in one last question before he left.

'This might sound stupid, but does the number 49 make any sense to you, perhaps in connection to the police.'

Walker eyes twinkled with amusement. 'You mean you never heard of the best of the best?'

Niven shook his head, tried to hide his excitement. Walker seemed to know something.

'No, don't suppose you would, son. He was before your time and far too simple for your generation, our PC 49. Things were more black and white when he was in his pomp.'

Niven had thrown out the question more in hope than anything else. Now he was eager to hear this.

'The suspense is killing me. Indulge me, please. Who was he?'

'PC 49 was a comic book hero back in the fifties, even had his own radio programme. He was an old-fashioned copper, the kind with the simple integrity you don't find very often in real life, more's the pity. I haven't heard him mentioned since I was a kid. What made you ask?'

'It's to do with one of the cases we're working on. This is in strict confidence but the suspect left a card at the crime scene with 49 printed on it. We know he was dressed as a policeman.'

'Blimey! Plenty of scope for the profilers and shrinks if there is a connection. They'll be telling you your man must think he's a hero righting wrongs, and puzzling over why he would return to the fifties to find an alter ego.' Walker chuckled. 'Maybe your suspect's just an old guy gone senile and wandering back to childhood to live out his memories of a comic-book hero.'

'Or a younger person who's heard about this character from an older man?' Niven mused. 'Whatever, it's a strange one!'

Walker stared at him. Niven thought he caught a gleam of

understanding in his eyes and worried he'd said too much. But the old copper put his mind at rest.

'Don't worry about it, son. My lips are sealed.'

Niven was pretty sure he would be true to his word. Thanking him for his patience, he rose to leave.

'You will try to find out about the widow and her children, won't you?' he said as he moved away from the table.

Walker touched his forelock. 'Consider it already done.'

Niven walked back to headquarters in fading light, mulling things over. The day had proved to be momentous though he felt he was in a twilight zone where past and present meet with nothing in focus. By the time he arrived back, he felt mentally drained and decided not to bother going into the office. Instead he got straight into his car and drove home.

Back at his flat, the first thing he did was ring the hospital, hoping the day would end with good news. The nurse who picked up gave him the answer he was growing accustomed to hearing and beginning to hate; Gill's condition showed no change from the last time. When he asked whether the items he'd brought in had helped, he was told Gill had been asleep or drowsy most of the day, hadn't yet returned to full cognizance.

He put the phone down, comforted himself with the knowledge that at least she hadn't relapsed. After making himself a mug of tea and a ham sandwich, he sat in the dark looking out to the horizon where the sun still lingered. He thought about the meeting with his mother. Gill had made their reunion possible, but at an awful price. Deeply touched by what she had done for him, his tears blurred the sun as it finally bowed its head in surrender to the night.

CHAPTER 32

Jack Cannon had no doubts about what he had to do. Terry had asked and that was good enough. Their mothers were sisters and they'd been brought up in each other's pockets, the principle of all for one and one for all was ingrained in him from childhood: you stood up for family against the world every time.

It helped that he had so little to lose. With a murder charge in prospect, plus his record of violence, he was sure to get a life sentence. What difference would one more killing make if he was caught? There wasn't much else they could do to him. Long term he'd try to escape. For now, he'd help his cousin avenge his son.

He was standing on the deserted landing looking down, observing the other inmates making the best of association before they were locked in their cells. Nobody was looking in his direction. He estimated around half the men on the floor below him were nonces who knew exactly how he felt about them, not so much by what he said but by his calculated coldness whenever one was near him. They knew what was good for them; they kept well clear of Jack Cannon.

It passed through his mind that, if only he'd resisted the temptation of a trip back to Middlesbrough to see an old girlfriend, he wouldn't have to suffer the indignity of being locked on the same wing with them, would be lying on a beach with the sun on his back now. He didn't dwell on it, though, because he wasn't a man to live too much in the past, or future, only in the moment. You took life as it came, did what you had to do without thought of consequence, without regret. That way no one could say you weren't a proper man.

From his vantage point he had a good view of the screws' office on the floor below. Except for the two who were walking the floors, all of them were inside. The walkers, he noted, were deep in conversation, not really attentive to their surroundings. He focused on the barred door to the wing. Micky Jones, Terry's pal, had taken up position close to it and was leaning casually against the wall, an arm's length stretch from the fire bell. Ostensibly he was reading a newspaper, but occasionally he would look up, check out Cannon. His pad was conveniently situated only feet away from that fire bell.

Cannon figured it was time. Paxton was in a cell several doors down from his own. Minutes earlier, he'd glanced inside, saw him flat out on his bed taking a siesta. He'd made a point of being extra friendly to Paxton, told him he'd been away so long he'd lost all ties with his family and resented the fact they appeared to have cut him out of their lives, acting as though he had no knowledge of bad blood between him and Terry. The fool had swallowed it, otherwise he wouldn't be so stupid as to lie there belly up, as defenceless as a beached whale.

He felt inside his pocket, extracted the plastic bag he'd snaffled from the kitchen, put his mind into a zone where he was so focused nothing was going to intervene between him and his task. Next time Micky glanced up, he stroked the back of his neck, the signal they'd agreed. He saw Micky tense. Then, as short and sharp as a boxer's jab, his arm shot out and his hand smashed into the glass face of the fire-alarm. Even as the alarm went off, like a rabbit scuttling into the sanctuary of its burrow, he disappeared into his pad.

As one, the cons stopped what they were doing, their heads turning towards the sound. The two screws walking the floor snapped out of their lethargy, ran towards the door and a moment later, like rugby forwards breaking from a scrum, their colleagues in the office burst out and charged blindly the same way. Cannon didn't stop to watch them because he needed to take full advantage of the time he had been given.

Long, unhurried strides propelled him to Paxton's cell where, as he entered, his target stirred on the bed. Cannon noticed his eyelids start to flicker, then his lips pout and vibrate as the noise of the alarm penetrated his slumber. But he never had a chance to fully awaken because Cannon leapt onto the bed, straddled him, pulled the plastic bag over his head and right down over his nose and mouth.

Under the plastic, Paxton's eyes sprang open. A momentary look of surprise gave way to one of terror beyond imagining. Like a wild horse trying to unseat its rider, he bucked and kicked to free himself. But it was wasted effort because Cannon was a much heavier, stronger man and easily pinned him down, the flailing arms not the slightest impediment as they deflected off his muscular frame.

When Paxton's eyes bulged so much that it seemed they would pop out of their sockets Cannon knew he was on his way out. He made one last effort to throw his attacker off, then his body convulsed and his head fell to the side. In the stillness of death, he was grotesque, his mouth wide open as though caught mid scream, his eyes trapped in a timeless horror.

No time to waste, grinning with satisfaction, Cannon leapt off the body, ran back onto the landing, closed the door and hurried back to his pad. The whole business hadn't taken him much more than two minutes and it only took him seconds to strip off and climb under his duvet where he would claim to have been when Paxton took his leave.

After the massive adrenalin rush, his breathing only gradually settled down. With luck, the body wouldn't be discovered until the end of association when the screws locked the prisoners back in their cells. Forensics would likely find traces of his presence in the cell, but other prisoners had been in there too and several cons had handled the plastic bag. Even if they could prove it was he who'd done it, it didn't much matter. Prison was going to be his home for a long time and killing a man under the noses of the screws wouldn't do his kudos any harm. On such acts respect was built, legends started. What harm?

CHAPTER 33

John Walker rang Niven at work the day after their meeting. He had been true to his word and had contacted his old colleagues. One of them had come up with the information that PC Thompson's widow hadn't remarried and was living alone in a house in Acklam, only a short drive from Headquarters.

That same morning Niven had informed DI Johnson he'd like to look into possible connections between Peacock, Paxton and Brannigan. Though he knew he should reveal his newly discovered relationship with the criminal, he couldn't do it, just told the DI he had a hunch that the clue to the killer's motive might lie in the three mens' shared history, but that he wasn't holding his breath. Johnson gave his consent, so his conscience was clear visiting the widow in work time as part of the investigation.

Within an hour of Walker's phone call, he was standing outside the house where the widow lived. Like most properties in Acklam it was well maintained and it seemed Mrs Thompson hadn't done too badly for herself, considering she must have brought up her children without a husband. Unfortunately, Walker hadn't managed to come up with any info about those children. Hopefully, their mother would enlighten him.

The woman with dyed blonde hair who answered the bell was in her early fifties. Evidently she was ready to go out because she was dressed in a bright red coat, wore red gloves and held a red plastic shopping bag. Blonde hair and alabaster skin provided a sharp contrast to her dress sense. Niven thought she could have passed for a female Santa Claus and obviously didn't mind standing out in a crowd. However, there was nothing of good cheer in her irritated expression, the way she looked him up and down as though he was the dog's left over dinner.

When he showed his ID and introduced himself, she grimaced, tilted her head back and rolled her eyes, reminded him of a spooked horse shying away from a jump it didn't like; he almost expected her to whinny. She couldn't have made her displeasure more obvious and he thought that didn't bode well.

'This is about my Alan, isn't it?' she snapped, before he could explain the purpose of his visit. 'Well, then, there's nothing I'm going to tell you except that he's a good lad and it's a disgrace what's happening to him. What's the world coming to when a little sewer rat can do that to a good man?'

Without him even having to ask, she'd just confirmed she had a son called Alan who was in trouble. It just had to be the teacher and that surely meant this could be a breakthrough. Niven felt a surge of excitement, wondered how he should play this.

'I'm not here about your Alan,' he said quietly, hoping she'd calm down.

She didn't seem to hear him, but warmed to her theme.

'Being on bail is torturing him, you know – all that waiting and wondering whether he'll go to jail! It's just not fair on a sensitive lad like my Alan.' She shook her head. 'He says he's coping, but a mother knows – a mother knows.'

She was silent for a moment, gathering breath and staring vacantly, as though, lost in her rant, she'd forgotten Niven was there. Then, that disdainful look returned and he realized she wasn't going to be easy, that he'd need to be diplomatic if he wanted co-operation.

'I know how you feel,' he agreed. 'Teachers have to put up

with so much provocation, don't they? It must take the patience of a saint to control yourself. I'm sure I would hit out.'

He hoped that would do the trick and it seemed to work because a softer look came into her eyes. Her facial muscles relaxed and her voice was an octave lower when she spoke.

'What is it you want from me, exactly?'

Niven summoned his best, ingratiating smile.

'I've been working on an old case, Mrs Thompson.'

He was thinking on his feet here, trying to judge how much he could tell her without alienating her.

'It was a case that involved your late husband and I think you might be the only one who can clear certain matters so I can put it to bed.'

Like a bird's wings arching just before it swoops towards its prey, her eyebrows shot up in unison and hovered. Finally, they descended into a frown, the glower returning. Niven was sure she was getting ready to roast him again and was relieved to find it was her dead husband, not he, who was the catalyst for her anger.

'Good God! Is there no escaping that man? Even from beyond the grave he has to harass me.'

Niven decided this was a moment to keep his counsel, let it ride. She was making it clear where she stood; anything he said now might light a blue touch paper. It proved a wise decision because she calmed down.

'I suppose you'd better come in for a minute,' she said, with a resigned sigh, 'though I can't see that anything I can say will be of any help. He's long dead and good riddance too.'

The living-room's décor surprised Niven. Given her sartorial tastes, he'd expected garishness, but it was much more conservative than her dress sense, the furniture for comfort rather than show. Had she a split personality, one for the outside world, one for the home, he wondered as she sat opposite him and folded her arms in a way that made the action like an act of defiance.

He let his eyes wander to the photographs of two boys that crowded the mantelpiece. He couldn't see their faces clearly, but guessed they had to be her sons. It gave him his opening.

'I take it those are your sons,' he said, pointing. 'They look fine figures, a credit to you.'

The woman visibly preened. 'Yes, they are. It was hard bringing them up on my own but, truth be told, it was easier without their father. Alan became a teacher and Brian a nurse.' She hesitated, a melancholy look coming into her eye. 'I just hope everything gets back to normal for Alan.'

Niven thought, while she'd not exactly warmed to him, she'd thawed considerably, so he decided to take the conversation into stormier waters.

'As I said, it's your husband I'm really here to talk about, Mrs Thompson.'

She scowled, the way only a person with a surfeit of bitterness can. It made her look older and ugly.

'He's been six foot under for a long time. Why would you want to know about him now?'

Niven improvised. 'I'm looking at cases where policemen claimed compensation for injury and weren't awarded. Your husband had a claim turned down but the paperwork isn't that clear. I'd like to know from you how he was at the time he left the force, his health, state of mind, things like that.'

Given the circumstances of her husband's death, he wasn't exactly comfortable with what he was doing. The saving grace was that he'd inquired about the period when her husband left the force, not about the suicide. Also, it was evident there'd been no love lost between them.

'Bit late, isn't it?' she said, laughing harshly. 'Unless they're going to reverse the decision, pay the compensation to his grieving widow. Chance would be a fine thing, eh?'

He shrugged his shoulders, implying he didn't know, leaving room for the possibility. His deceit made him a little ashamed, but he thought it might be an incentive for her to open up about her husband. He'd much rather have got right down to it, but she was touchy and he could see a more direct approach could well alienate her. As it was, he felt he was walking a tightrope, that one wrong question could set her against him.

'I know this can't be pleasant for you,' he said, 'but I'd really like to know if there were noticeable differences in your husband's behaviour after the robbery, after that blow he took.'

The woman threw back her head, cackled like a witch.

'He wasn't up to much before or after the robbery, my husband. He had these mood changes, you see.' She angled her head, stared doubtfully at him. 'If you've done your research, you'll know he was taking drugs while he was serving. That made his moods worse. After he left your lot, he started taking more drugs.'

'So you don't think the moods were the result of his being beaten by those robbers?'

'The doctor didn't think so, did he? He was fool enough to have drugs in his bloodstream at the time they examined him, you know.'

'I didn't know, must have missed that,' he lied. 'Did these mood changes of his affect your boys?'

He'd gone the long way round, but was getting closer to the subject he wanted answers on, hopefully without her realizing the road he was taking.

Her eyes moistened. She took a deep breath before she answered.

'I told them their father had been hurt on duty and that was why he could turn funny. He beat me often, but fortunately never when they were there and he was clever enough never to hit my face.'

Niven felt sorry for the woman. An experience like that left its mark and it was obvious she had been deeply affected. Regretting that his questions must be reviving old hurts, but knowing they were necessary, he pressed on.

'So your boys never knew what kind of a man their father was, nor about his drugs?'

From her pained look, Niven thought he'd pushed her too far; he had been prodding a festering wound. He sat there on tenterhooks, hoping she wouldn't tell him to go to hell.

'They didn't know what he was like,' she snorted, eventually. 'The poor mites were only ten and twelve years old when everything blew apart. He told them stories and he was always the hero. His version of the robbery was he'd fought three men and was so badly hurt he had to stop being a policeman – all a fiction of course.'

She paused, fingers tapping on the arms of her chair, lips set in a grimace.

'It made me sick, but I went along with it, thinking it was better they thought something of their father rather than know the truth – that he was a drug-addicted bully.'

'It was the kindest thing to do, a brave thing,' Niven said, meaning it.

She lowered her head, stared down at the floor as though lost in a past of regrets. Then, she spoke again.

'All I know is, after believing he was a big hero, the truth would have been shattering for them and might have damaged my boys.' A moment's hesitation and she added, 'He hung himself, didn't he? Imagine what that was like for them.'

Niven was glad it was she who'd broached that particular subject. As a boy, on those occasions he'd speculated about his real father, he often imagined him as a heroic figure. It had never entered his head he could be a criminal. Finding the truth had been shattering for him as an adult. They'd only been boys, her sons.

'Believe me, I can imagine.'

'They were devastated,' she continued, 'but even then I lied for him, told them it was because of the pain he was suffering due to that beating he'd taken. So you see even in death he remained a hero to them.'

Niven was seeing her in a new light. Was that garish dress sense an act of defiance, over-compensating for a downtrodden past lived in the grey shadows of a sham marriage? She should have had the courage to leave her husband, but it seemed she had chosen to stay because of a misguided notion any father was better than none. In her own way, she'd shown the strength of a mother's love for her children.

He forced his mind back to practical matters. Alan Thompson, he now knew, had good reason to hate the three villains. Perhaps his trouble at school turned his mind, brought back old resentments and made him decide, however belatedly, to avenge his father. Could the teacher be the killer policeman, the uniform connecting him, in his warped mind, to his father and those stories of his heroism?

'This might sound foolish,' he said, clearing his throat. 'But have you ever heard of a PC 49?'

She stared at him as though he was a mystic who'd looked into her soul and seen all the secrets residing there. Her hand flew to her heart.

'My God! How could you possibly know?'

Her reaction left no doubt that PC 49 struck a chord. He kept the excitement out of his voice.

'What exactly do you think I know, Mrs Thompson?'

She flopped back in the chair, her eyes blinking.

'When my husband told the boys his tall tales, he called himself PC 49, after a character in a comic book.' She shook her head in puzzlement. 'I don't understand. How could you know unless my sons told you about him?'

Niven didn't know how to answer. His hunch was turning into reality; it seemed within the bounds of possibility that Alan Thompson had become PC 49 incarnate, in that guise set out to take vengeance for his father. But how could he voice those suspicions to his mother? She wouldn't believe him anyway.

'I didn't hear it from your sons.'

Niven's stomach churned as he waited for her to react, hoping she wouldn't press him further on the matter.

'My God!' she said. 'It's like being haunted. Never thought I'd hear PC 49 again. Never wanted to! I grew sick and tired of those stories he told.' She looked at Niven accusingly. 'I thought he was buried with my husband and good riddance to them both.'

'Sorry I had to resurrect them for you,' he muttered.

He had other questions, but didn't want to arouse her suspicions. It was time to leave well alone. She'd likely have to suffer later without his causing her needless distress. Anyway, he had plenty of avenues to pursue now.

'I've taken enough of your time.' he said, rising. 'Best I get on my way. You've been a great help.'

She followed him to the door. When they faced each other, he thought she looked older, as though excavating her unpleasant past had added years to her age. She was looking at him in a way that made him think she'd seen through his subterfuge, worked out for herself there were things he wasn't saying.

'Could I ask you a favour, detective?' Her voice was not far short of pleading.

'What's that, Mrs Thompson?'

'See if there's anything you can do to help my Alan. He doesn't deserve what's happening to him.'

He forced a smile, aware of the sad irony: asking help from a man who was possibly going to send her son to jail for a long time.

'I'll see what I can do,' he mumbled.

He hated the lie even as it passed his lips and, reaching out to shake her hand, he felt like a con artist. Going down the path, he felt her eyes trained on his back, was glad when he was out of sight. No doubt she'd helped him make a massive breakthrough today but no way could he feel good about the way he'd used her against her son.

*

Alan Thompson had watched Niven coming up the path and scuttled upstairs. He caught brief snatches of the conversation with his mother on the doorstep and had been relieved to hear the detective declare his visit wasn't to do with him. After that, he'd no idea what passed in the living-room, but was relieved when Niven left the house. Only when the detective was out of sight, did he venture downstairs.

'What was that about?' he asked his mother.

'It wasn't about you,' she told him, 'but next time it might be. You need to go back to you flat, son. I don't want you to make things worse for yourself.'

He leaned against the banister. His mother was right of course; he couldn't stay there any longer breaking the terms of his bail. He'd been so miserable alone in his flat he'd headed home the way a wounded animal heads for an old den it thinks safe, a place to lick its wounds. Though he'd hated burdening her, his mother had listened sympathetically and it had helped him to pour it all out. Part of him was afraid he might go mad.

He followed his mother into the kitchen and put the kettle on.

'You're right, Mum,' he said. 'Got to get myself together and face it. Can't hide here forever behind your skirts.'

She turned towards him, smiled sadly. 'It's not that I want you to go. It's just that it's best for you.'

He put an arm around her shoulder. 'So what did the man want? No need to hide it from me, Mum. I know he's a detective. He was one of the policemen who interviewed me and I was sure he must have come about my case.'

She shook her head. 'He said he was looking at old cases when policemen failed to receive compensation, so wanted to know about your father. He was a nice man really, quite sensitive.'

Alan frowned. It seemed to him Niven had given her a cock and bull story. But why? To gain entry to the house to see if there were any signs of him living there? That seemed unlikely somehow.

'I told him all about your father,' his mother volunteered, breaking into his thoughts, 'and the strangest thing was, out of the blue, he asked if I'd heard of PC 49.'

'Forget about it, Mum,' he said, surprised. 'It can't mean anything, can it? Just a bizarre coincidence. You go out and do your shopping. I'll have your tea ready when you come in.'

She picked up her bag and smiled at him.

'You're a good lad, Alan,' she said. 'You don't deserve what's happened to you.'

CHAPTER 34

Parked a little way down the road from the widow's house, Niven sank back in the seat and ran through what he'd learned, fitting the pieces together so that there was hardly a rough edge showing. No doubt about it, he had enough information to put to DI Johnson. And Alan Thompson was going to have to defend himself concerning a much more serious matter than assaulting a pupil. His boss would be relieved they were getting somewhere.

He slid the key into the ignition, intending to drive straight back to headquarters. Before he set off, though, he remembered he'd left his mobile in the glove compartment, checked it for messages and found one from Clem Davis at Stockton Prison. The security officer's voice sounded flat as he told how they'd searched Brannigan's pad, but found no mobile phone, even flatter when, after a resigned sigh, he informed Niven that Don Paxton had been found dead in his cell, a plastic bag over his head. The investigation was ongoing, but it was pretty clear it wasn't suicide. The message concluded with Clem saying that, if Niven needed more information, he should call him.

Niven drooped his arms over the top of steering wheel, feeling deflated. Don Paxton's death fitted with the idea that the three robbers were the killer's targets but, unless he was able to pass through walls, how could Alan Thompson have done it?

Terry Brannigan was a better candidate. There was bad blood between him and the dead man and they were both incarcerated. But why, so near to release, knowing if he was caught he'd get life, would he go to that extreme? Could he be underestimating Alan Thompson? Had the teacher more guile than his demeanour suggested, enough perhaps to manipulate someone on the inside into doing his work for him?

Niven remembered the sympathy he'd felt for the teacher's plight. Thompson picked up on it fast, his manner becoming familiar, which spooked Niven at the time. Making the call informing him Gill was hurt, he remembered the killer spoke with that same, assumed intimacy. But all this was getting him precisely nowhere. The main question was, could Thompson have got to Paxton.

Back at Headquarters, he parked up, sat debating whether he should ring the prison to tell them everything he knew, or suspected? Brannigan could well be next for termination, but he'd feel foolish suggesting he was in danger from the schoolteacher. It seemed ironic he was having to concern himself with the welfare of his birth father, a man he didn't know from Adam. Finally he decided, whether he'd feel foolish or not, he should follow his conscience.

Clem Davis answered his call and Niven didn't mess about, got straight to the point.

'There're things you should know, Clem. Take too long to go into it all but I think Jimmy Peacock and Don Paxton were targets for someone seeking revenge and next on his list is their pal Brannigan.'

There was a moment's silence on the other end. Niven waited, a good idea what was coming.

'But Paxton was killed in here, Peacock outside the prison? Doesn't make a lot of sense that it's the same man responsible, does it?'

'Maybe someone on the inside is working with him, I don't know. The man I fancy for it has no previous and no contact with the criminal world as far as I know.'

'There are people in here would kill their grannies for money, no questions asked.'

'I know that. It's possible my man paid someone, but I doubt he has that kind of contact, or the money for that matter. Just be aware something could be in the wind, Clem.'

Niven heard the security officer sigh. 'Well, you weren't far off the mark warning us Paxton was in trouble and I'm afraid we made a pig's ear there. Brannigan will be going to his son's funeral tomorrow. Don't think I can stop that or get much extra manpower, but at least we're forewarned.'

'Hope I'm not barking up the wrong tree, but forewarned is forearmed!'

On that final note, content he had at least complied with the demands of his conscience, Niven ended the call.

CHAPTER 35

Paxton's death didn't merit much space in the evening paper. PC read it with a smile of satisfaction as he recalled the way he had manipulated Brannigan. How easy had that been?

Two down, one to go! He was sitting in his car a little way along the road from Darren's house, ready to begin the last stage of his quest. It would be audacious, but he had an advantage in not caring how it turned out for himself as long as Brannigan, the third of the triumvirate, was brought to justice. Besides, going out in a flourish, standing on his own two feet like a man, appealed to him.

He put aside the paper, picked up the bunch of flowers lying on the passenger seat. Two minutes later, he was at he dead man's door mustering a suitably sombre expression. The girl who answered his knock was pretty enough, but had a sleepy, vacant look which, even allowing for the fact she was grieving, suggested she wasn't the brightest. Hopefully, that would work to his advantage.

'You must be Darren's lady,' he said, cocking his head to one side, manufacturing what he hoped was a sympathetic smile.

'Yeah, I am,' she muttered, pushing back a strand of loose hair, eyes alighting on the flowers as though she'd never seen any before, her gaze remaining there rather than on her visitor.

'I'm so sorry about Darren,' he said, holding the flowers out. 'He was an old pal and I've only just heard. These are for you Barbara. It is Barbara, isn't it?'

She nodded, took the flowers without any show of gratitude,

holding them loosely against her leg. A silence ensued and he decided he would wait for her to say something first.

'You knew my Darren, like,' she managed eventually, eyes blinking as though it was difficult for her to keep him in focus. She looked about as vivacious as a doped up sloth and he hoped, if drugs were the cause of her passivity, she wasn't so far gone she couldn't give him what he wanted.

'We were muckers a few years back, but I've been away, just got back.' He dropped his voice. 'Someone told me Darren had been – murdered. I was ... shocked.'

'The funeral's tomorrow,' she stated, her voice flat although at last deigning to look him in the face, though more through him than at him. He didn't care because all that mattered was she'd volunteered one piece of information he'd wanted from her.

'I'd like to attend the funeral, if that would be all right. Pay my respects.'

She shrugged as though it was a matter of indifference to her what he did.

'It's at St Andrew's Church, quarter-to-twelve.'

So far so good, he thought; it had taken no effort to ascertain the time and place. Now only one piece of information, the most crucial, remained, and he was direct about asking for it.

'Terry will be there, I suppose?'

His question brought a sign of life into those sheep's eyes, but it was only a brief spark conveying irritation.

'He'll be there,' she moaned, not disguising her displeasure at the prospect. 'You a friend of his, like?'

He thought quickly. 'I know him but he's more of an acquaintance, really.'

'Well, him and me don't get on, see. I've asked the vicar to make sure he's put well away from me – him and all his guards.'

'I can understand, pet. Takes the dignity of the occasion away, doesn't it? The vicar will understand that. What's his name by the way, the vicar?' He knew he was a being bit too curious, but she was so obviously distracted by the thought of Brannigan's presence at the funeral it was worth the chance.

'Holt. Reverend Holt, 'she answered, without hesitation. 'He says I can sit anywhere I like. Don't have to sit with Terry if I don't want.'

'He's right, darling. It's a free country. No different in a church.'

He was smiling inwardly because she'd given him everything he wanted. Now all that remained was to take his leave so, making a show of looking at his watch, he edged away. In her own world again, she hardly seemed to notice his retreat.

'You take care of yourself,' he called out. 'Sorry about Darren. He was sound.'

She didn't say anything. When he reached the gate and looked back, she was standing there with that same hangdog expression she'd had when he arrived, the flowers dangling in her hand with their heads drooping as though they'd caught her mood and come out in sympathy. For a fleeting moment he felt sorry for her, not for her loss, but because she didn't have the mental acumen, or whatever it took, to realize she'd have a better life away from families like the Brannigans.

Half an hour later, he was back in his flat, sitting at the kitchen table, a letter pad on the table, a pen in his hand. When he died tomorrow, he wanted those close to him to know why he had departed in the manner he had chosen for himself. Words committed to paper were the best way to do that because they left no room for doubt.

In the letter he explained how his faith in a greater purpose behind even the most savage of acts had withered, becoming a mere flicker of hope. This hope, he continued, was all he had to face acts like the one those three criminals had committed against his father and, he had come to realize, this wasn't enough. He wanted certainties, to be sure that justice for his father would prevail here and now. He'd been late in coming to that conclusion, but better late than never. Finally he told his family he loved them and hoped they'd forgive him for risking his eternal soul.

It took him two hours to finish the letters, to choose the words to express his feelings. In time, the recipients might come to understand how he was feeling. Tomorrow, he'd deliver the letters. By the time they were read, it would all be done and dusted.

CHAPTER 36

The vicarage was an austere building set in a spacious garden. Tall trees secluded it from prying eyes. PC had known the building since he was a boy. He left the hire van on the road, wandered up the driveway quite satisfied that his dyed, black hair and horn rimmed spectacles were a convincing disguise. When he'd looked in the mirror that morning, he'd hardly recognized the person staring back at him.

The plump woman who answered was in her dressing gown. She stifled a yawn, summoned a smile which failed to hide a trace of irritation in her eyes. He supposed she was put out being disturbed at such an unchristian hour. Well, then, she was going to find herself more put out than she could ever have imagined.

'Is this the Reverend Holt's abode, my dear,' he said, playing the role of charming eccentric.

She hesitated, not quite sure of this stranger on her doorstep.

'Actually he's just started his breakfast. Is it—'

'Important?' he said, cutting in. 'Yes, it is, a matter of great concern, life and death I should say.'

Clearly intrigued, but not sure of him yet, she hesitated then gave him a cool, appraising look that measured him from top to toe. Just as he thought he was going to have to resort to strong-arm tactics, she stepped back and held the door open for him.

'If that's the case you'd better come in and speak to my husband.'

He followed her down a long hallway where paintings of

religious scenes left no doubt that the house was a vicarage. The vicar was in the living-room sitting at a table near the window. His grey hair was uncombed and he wore a ludicrous, pink dressing-gown with floral patterns. Focused on a newspaper and biting absent mindedly into a piece of toast, he didn't notice them for a moment. Then, he looked up, realized he had a visitor and gave a start. Looking rather abashed, he put his paper down and, wiping his mouth with a napkin, rose to his feet. Considering that feminine dressing gown, which surely had to be one of his wife's and did nothing to dignify him, it was no wonder his face was red.

'This gentleman wants to speak with you, my dear.' The wife glanced doubtfully at PC. 'He says it's a matter of life and death, otherwise I wouldn't have disturbed you.'

The reverend's eyebrows knitted into a frown. He had recovered some of his composure, but his down-turned mouth and bad tempered look seemed to indicate it was far too early in the morning for the practice of Christian charity – or to be caught cross dressing.

'So, an errand concerning life and death, is it?' he echoed, accompanying it with a supercilious tilt of his head that implied he was sure, whatever it was, that must be an exaggeration.

'Yes, actually, that's just what it is, and whether life wins over death will be in your own hands. Given your profession, who could be more worthy?'

With that, PC pulled his gun from his pocket and grabbed the woman by the arm. She opened her mouth as though she was about to scream, but was so terrified no sound emerged past her lips. For his part, her husband recoiled and grasped the chair to steady himself. Satisfied they were under his spell, PC manoeuvred the wife towards the table.

'Sit down!' he ordered. 'Both of you!'

Exchanging frightened glances and transfixed by the gun, they did as they were told like zombies.

'Now we're cosy let me make this clear,' PC told them. 'It's as simple as sin really. If you do exactly as you're told you'll live through this. If you don't—'

The wife started to bubble. Her husband snapped out of his stupor to reach across the table for her hand. His other hand was trembling.

'Why?' he said, voice barely more than a whisper. 'Why are you doing this? We haven't done anything to you.'

PC smiled indulgently.

'Innocent lambs are sacrificed in the Bible, aren't they? All over the world innocents are dying as we speak. Being a man of the Church doesn't grant immunity from such things, does it?' He raised his eyes heavenward. 'If it makes it easier for you, just believe I can hear a voice in my head telling me what I have to do. You know, like Moses.'

The woman let out a wail while her husband blanched.

'This voice,' the vicar gulped. 'It's telling you to ... kill us?'

'Only if you don't obey!'

PC was secretly amused. They believed he was off the wall enough to do what he threatened, which was exactly what he wanted them to believe.

A gleam entered the vicar's eye but he was ahead of him, knew he was thinking he might be able to use his intellect to manipulate this intruder who imagined he heard voices. When he pointed the gun in his direction, the gleam instantly disappeared.

'I'm going to perform Darren Brannigan's funeral which means you're going to take the day off, vicar.'

'Why on earth—?'

PC made a show of glancing at his watch.

'We're operating on a need-to-know basis here and all you need to know is you have an hour to acquaint me with the format of the service.'

'But it's sacrilege,' the vicar protested. 'How could you explain to anyone ... People will expect me—'

'No they won't. You've taken ill. Luckily another vicar was visiting and he graciously agreed to step in for you at the last minute.'

The vicar shook his head. 'Surely you don't think you can fool a whole congregation?'

'Faith can move mountains, can't it?'

The vicar didn't reply, seeming to shrink into himself. PC turned to his wife. She had covered her face with her hands, was peeping from between her fingers.

'Your good wife will accompany me. I'll leave her somewhere safe and there'll be a note in the vestry telling you where that is. If you start anything before two hours have passed there can be no guarantees your wife will be found.'

The woman slid her hands away from her face, dried the tears in her eyes with a handkerchief. PC was surprised when she took the initiative.

'We have to do what he says, dear. We've no choice.'

The vicar heaved a sigh of frustration. 'You promise not to hurt her?'

'Yes, unless there's a Judas in the house!'

He stared at his wife, his anguish showing in his face.

'There's no rhyme or reason to what you're doing. I beg you to think again.'

PC shook his head. 'Just do as you're told and go and get me everything I need, the full panoply, surplice, dog-collar, order of service.'

The vicar rose, his mouth curling in distaste.

'Go on,' PC told him. 'She'll be fine. She'll only come to harm if you fail to follow orders.'

He trudged out of the room, soon returned with the accoutrements of his trade he'd been ordered to fetch. PC immediately tried on the surplice and dog-collar and found them quite a good fit. But he knew it was one thing to look the part, another to perform it. He pointed to the briefcase on the table.

'I take it my script is in there. I need you to go through it with me.'

His face white with anger, the vicar opened the clasp, extracted various papers and pamphlets and laid them in a pile on the table.

'We'll start with the general order of the service first, then consider the detail,' PC told him.

It took them twenty minutes to run through it, PC asking questions he thought relevant. Fortunately, it appeared there would be only one speaker other than himself, a friend of Darren's who wanted to say a few words.

'Is there anything else you should tell me,' PC asked when they were done. 'It's in your interests as well as mine that I conduct the service without raising any suspicions.'

The wife chirped up, 'My husband can ring the organist to explain what's happening. He'll let the ushers know. Once you're at the church, the only person you need to speak to is the organist.'

PC focused on the vicar. 'Nobody will bother me in the vestry?'

'No, I keep that as my private domain – for reflection – before and after a service.'

PC grinned. 'Means you can have a go at the communion wine without being disturbed, I suppose. Now, have you told me everything?'

'There's nothing else,' the vicar said, his voice flat.

'Good! That's us done then. All you do is stay at home, read the Ecumenical Times or whatever.' He turned to the wife. 'Don't worry my dear, as long as hubby doesn't do anything foolish while you're away you'll survive this horrible experience.'

Ten minutes later, PC and the woman stepped onto the drive together. The vicar, his pretty dressing gown wrapped around him, watched from the door as they walked down the drive.

'Say a prayer,' PC called over his shoulder. 'It might just work.'

*

The wife sat silently in the passenger seat, her back rigid as he drove the white hire van through the outskirts of town to the disused factory he'd selected because it was well hidden from prying eyes. When he parked and ordered her out, her courage failed her and she couldn't move herself.

'Listen,' he said, hoping he wouldn't have to get rough. 'I'm not a bad man and nothing is going to happen to you. The whole point is your husband has to think it might. I'm going to tie you up in the back now, drive to a street near the church and leave you there. The hire firm has been told to collect the vehicle from that precise position in a few hours time. The note I'm going to leave is double insurance you'll be found. Can't say fairer than that, can I?'

He thought she looked reassured but then the doubt returned in her eyes and she started to sob. Grabbing her arms, he shook her hard until she became perfectly still.

'Trust me,' he said. 'I don't like doing this to you. You're not my target.'

This time his words had an effect. She stared at the derelict factory building with its shattered windows, graffiti decorated walls, at the rubble strewn landscape.

'You're going to hurt someone, aren't you? I just know you are. That gun – if you're not an evil person why are you doing this?'

'It's too long a story and you wouldn't understand,' he said. 'Now, please get out and go to the back of the van.'

This time she complied. When he opened the doors, she climbed in and lay on the mattress he'd placed inside for her, didn't move a muscle as he trussed her up tightly.

Before he gagged her, he whispered, 'Sorry! Forgive me!'

Closing the back doors, he returned to the driver's seat, satisfied that so far everything had gone to plan.

CHAPTER 37

Niven sat across the desk from his boss. Johnson looked grey and careworn, an extra flap of flab under his chin suggesting he'd been comfort eating again. There was a certain, uncharacteristic lassitude in his manner too, but he revived when Niven told him about his visit to Mrs Thompson, how everything seemed to point to Alan Thompson as the killer with a motive.

'A schoolteacher!' Johnson said, incredulous. 'Our man's a schoolteacher?'

'Can't be absolutely certain but it looks that way, sir?'

'It does, it does.' Johnson pursed his lips. 'But if what you say is true why would he wait all these years to exact revenge?'

Niven shrugged. He'd been wondering about that himself and could only hypothesize.

'I'm no psychologist but we know his career has just gone down the spout big time. That could have affected his mental state, brought back bad memories. Maybe he thinks he's getting back at society for what happened to his father and now to him.'

Johnson mulled it over. 'It's possible, I suppose. My sister's a teacher. She says that with some of the brats in school these says it's a wonder more teacher's don't flip.'

'Thompson's out on bail, sir, reports every morning. What will we do?'

'Don't wait for him, go and bring him in! What we've got is mainly circumstantial, but it's pretty damning. We need to face him with it, see if he breaks.'

'He lives in a flat not that far from his mother. How do you want me to play it, sir?'

Johnson rubbed his hands together as though he was contemplating a feast set in front of him after starving for far too long.

'Take enough men to surround the place. We don't want him slipping away.'

Niven rose, started to say something, but changed his mind. When he was at the door, Johnson called out to him.

'Great initiative by the way. Joining all those dots was detective work of the highest standard.'

Niven flushed. The praise was undeserved. If only Johnson knew what had motivated him!

'The ball just started rolling the right way for me.'

Johnson grinned. 'Take credit where it's due, son. There'll be plenty of those other times.'

Outside the office, he felt ashamed leaving his boss in the dark like that. The ball had indeed started to roll for him, but only because he'd been curious to learn about his criminal father, a fact he'd neglected to mention. He'd steeled himself to confide in Johnson but, when push had come to shove, just couldn't do it.

He was aware the longer he left it the harder it would be to confess. Of course, he could just let it lie. After all, Brannigan hadn't played any part in his life. But he knew that was just an excuse. It was his duty to declare any familial relationship with a criminal and it rankled with him that he hadn't found it in himself to do so.

The marked police cars followed Niven to the road where Alan Thompson resided. He parked a little way from the flats and waited until the uniforms joined him. Deciding to play safe, he gave orders that one car should go to the road behind the flats just in case Thompson did a runner. The other would park out front while he and two designated men entered to confront the teacher.

He rang the bell several times without any response, stooped to look through the letter box, saw the pile of mail on the floor which could only have accumulated over several days. Though the teacher had reported in regularly, it had been part of the terms of his bail that he remained at the same address. Judging by that mail, he wasn't keeping to that condition. Disappointed at a fruitless journey, Niven led his men back outside.

Knowing the value of keeping good relations with the uniforms, he apologized for the wasted trip, then got on the radio to arrange for patrols to drive past and check at regularly intervals in case Thompson returned. That done, he set off back to report to Johnson.

Returning via Grove Hill, he had to stop for an old man tottering over a crossing and noticed the cars parked bumper to bumper on the other side of the road outside St Andrew's Church. Further down the road, two police cars were parked up.

He remembered his last conversation with the prison security chief. Clem Davis had mentioned Darren Brannigan's funeral would be held today. This church was the closest to Darren's home and, therefore, surely a strong candidate for the funeral service. Chances were Brannigan senior would be inside.

The old man reached the other side of the road, raised his stick in thanks. Niven, concentrating on the church and lost in thought, only moved on when someone blasted their horn at him. A hundred yards further on, he came to a mini roundabout, instead of going straight across went right round and headed back the way he'd come. After all, he told himself, who wouldn't be curious for a peek at the man responsible for bringing him into the world.

CHAPTER 38

PC looked out of the narrow vestry window thinking of all those vicars who'd been there before him. He could feel the building's antiquity in his bones. Generations must have come here to worship, but he was certain they would never have witnessed anything like the commotion he intended to create. He heard the organ strike up, notes ascending to the heights, plunging and rising again. The nerves in his stomach seemed attuned to their rise and fall.

A phone call from the Reverend Holt had been enough to deceive the elderly organist. When they'd briefly shaken hands, he'd been nervous about his disguise, but it must have been pretty good because the organist hadn't shown a flicker of suspicion. Neither had the two ushers.

Moments ago he'd popped into the nave to count heads, figured there were around twenty present. He'd noticed Terry Brannigan was sitting in the front row, handcuffed to two burly prison officers. The criminal had been staring straight ahead and couldn't have been more than a few feet away from the pulpit where PC had hidden one of his guns. He supposed he could have done the business then and there. But he wanted Brannigan to know why he was going to die and those present to know why he'd turned man-hunter, that he wasn't just a wanton killer.

From the vestry window, he watched the sleek, black funeral cars glide up to the kerb, four men lift the coffin from the hearse, hoist it onto their shoulders and carry it towards the church door. The climax of all he'd worked for was so near now. All that remained was to go out and embrace his destiny.

Taking a deep breath, he stepped out of the vestry, assumed the air of a man self possessed enough to believe he had answers to the things that troubled men's hearts. As he ascended the pulpit and looked down on the congregation, he hoped his disguise and authoritative air would be enough to convince them. When the coffin entered the church, the organ grew more sombre and the bearers, marching in time with it, carried the coffin to the altar before retreating with their heads bowed.

PC came down from the pulpit, stood behind the coffin and raised his head. This was a critical moment; if anyone suspected he was an impostor, there'd be an immediate hue and cry. He sweated on those first few seconds, half expecting a voice to cry out and denounce him. But all he heard was Darren's girlfriend sobbing like a cat in pain. Voice rising to the rafters, he began.

'Man that is born of woman hath but a short time to live.'

Soon he was in full flow, his confidence growing. If he could hold his nerve, stick to the order of the service, he was sure everything would work out exactly as he wanted it to.

He joined heartily in the two hymns, affected solemn empathy as one of Darrren's friends made a garbled, inane speech, the gist of which was that his pal 'weren't no saint, a bit of a scallywag really, but always there for his mates'.

Finally, it was his turn to speak again. He stepped forward, stood behind the coffin, pleased the acting was over and that from now on every word he spoke would be from his heart.

'The death of someone we love is painful.'

He paused there, let his eye wander over the congregation before continuing. 'And today, above all things, I am remembering my own father's premature demise, the way he was so cruelly taken from me.'

The congregation shifted restlessly in the pews, most of them clearly uncomfortable with his personal indulgence. A few seemed to have missed it entirely, just looked bored, already wishing it was time for a post funeral booze-up.

'I can see you wondering,' he continued, 'what possible relevance my father's death has today.' Chest expanding visibly, he drew in a great breath. 'Well, then, rest assured, there is a strong link to these – proceedings – because the same man was involved in both deaths.'

A whisper started, swept through the congregation. Heads turned seeking affirmation. Had they heard correctly? He raised an arm, commanded their silence. Then, like an old time, fire-brand preacher, eyes aflame with righteous indignation, he pointed straight at Brannigan.

'Evil resides in that beast,' he shouted. 'He killed my father and his machinations killed his own son.'

As though the power of his invective had stilled the air itself, there was a stunned silence. Before anyone had a chance to challenge him, the gun appeared from under his surplice and he stepped down from the pulpit. Standing over the prisoner, who looked at him with contemptuous indifference, he aimed the weapon at his head and ordered the guards to uncuff him. Stupefied, the guards were slow to react until one of them snapped out of it. Producing a key from his pocket, he unlocked the handcuffs.

'Everybody leave! Now!'

Most members of the congregation rose to their feet at his command, squeezed out of the pews and hurried down the aisle, anxious to be out of there as quickly as possible. A minority, bunched together like sheep, made their way out more slowly. The guards were hesitant, not sure what he wanted them to do.

'Get out, both of you!' PC hissed, his eyes on Brannigan who returned his stare like a cornered animal waiting for its chance to spring.

The guards didn't need a second bidding and hurried away down the aisle, his voice following them.

'Tell the police not to try enter if they don't want a massacre on their hands.'

Niven showed his credentials to the uniformed officer who intercepted him at the church gate and slipped into the building, closing the door so quietly that the ushers didn't hear him. Neither did they notice him slide forward behind the column of pillars that ran down the side of the church. Hidden in the shadows, he spotted the uniformed guards in the front pew, a broad shouldered man with black, graying hair – Brannigan – their equal in bulk, sandwiched between them. Who else could the meat in the sandwich be but his blood father?

The service was already underway, the vicar in the middle of announcing a friend of Darren's wanted to say a few words. Something in his voice wheedled its way into the detective's memory. He was nearly sure he'd heard it before, but he just couldn't place it and, as he focused on the man himself, it niggled at him.

He didn't recognize the vicar, though, and was beginning to think he must be mistaken about the voice when, suddenly, its owner turned his head in his direction and he caught a fleeting glimpse of the eyes behind the heavy framed spectacles. Now he was really puzzled. Those eyes seemed familiar too.

Darren's pal finished his babbling and the vicar said something about the same man being responsible for Darren's and his own father's death. The detective heard the shock waves pass through the congregation when he accused Brannigan of killing his father, drew a gun which had been hidden and pointed it at the prisoner, ordering the congregation to leave.

Finally, Niven knew where he'd seen those blue eyes before and heard that voice. He was sure the vicar was Alan Thompson in disguise, that this was his final act of revenge for his father. Stepping back into the shadows, he watched the mourners scuttle down the aisle, the two guards following behind them. Brannigan was sure to die unless he could do something. But what could he do against an armed, fanatical man who had already proved he had no compunction about killing.

CHAPTER 39

PC and the criminal faced each other, eyes locked, waves of hate emanating from both men.

'So you're the scum who killed my Darren,' the criminal snarled.

'And you're the bastard who killed my father. At least with Darren it was quick.'

Brannigan half rose. 'You're crazy – a lunatic!'

PC pointed the gun at his head.

'Remember the post office raid in Nunthorpe, the policeman you beat up that day? That was my father. He went through torture because of what you and your scum did to him. When the pain was too much to bear he killed himself.'

Brannigan's eyes narrowed. 'If that druggy was your father, we did the world a favour.'

PC's face contorted. 'He was no druggy. He was a policeman!'

Brannigan threw back his head, laughed, not with mirth, but with a malice aimed at the man who'd killed his son.

'Your father was known in my world. He was a dirty, drug-dealing copper who could be bought with drugs.' His face grew uglier. 'So that's the man my son died for, the worst kind of copper, the kind that plays both sides?'

PC was incandescent. His arm started to tremble. This wasn't the way he'd planned his finale. Brannigan should have been on his knees by now, begging for mercy. Instead, he was manufacturing evil lies. He didn't want him to die with those lies on his lips. He had to be made to understand the magnitude of his sin, that he had destroyed a good man, left his wife a widow, deprived two sons of a father.

'Go on, do it,' Brannigan said. 'I don't care any more and there's no way out of this for you. Darren and me will be together but they'll put you away for the rest of your days. Believe me, for someone like you that'll be a hell worse than dying.'

His lack of contrition angered PC, but he was feeling weary from his exertions now. The time had come to end the talking and put an end to the criminal.

'There'll be no prison for me, Brannigan! The police are going to find both our bodies right here. If there's a hell, we'll meet there soon.'

Brannigan gazed into the gun barrel, shook his head.

'If that's to be, the devil himself won't stop me finding you, so do your worst.'

Niven stepped out from the shadows and started towards the two men at the altar, his footsteps echoing on the stone floor like a drumbeat accompanying a condemned man to the gallows.

As their heads swivelled, he kept walking. Appearing out of nowhere had at least given him the advantage of surprise, but he knew it wouldn't last. He needed to seize the initiative, shock the killer. Perhaps only the truth would do that and, anyway, he didn't have any other weapon but the truth.

'Brannigan is right,' he announced. 'Your father's drug-dealing was the reason he was forced to leave the police and his drug-taking contributed to his hanging himself. It wasn't anything to do with the injury he sustained. You've been protected from the truth all this time.'

When he'd got over his initial surprise, PC's scowl was uglier than a gargoyle's. Niven could see he'd got to him.

'You're lying!' he snapped. 'If you talk about my father like that I'll put a bullet in you as well.'

Niven tasted bile. The man was clearly unstable, but he couldn't change tack now, would have to sail into the eye of the storm.

'I've been to see your mother. She told me the truth, how she allowed you to believe he was a good man because she wanted you to look up to him, the way kids look up to their father.'

'Shut up!' PC yelled. 'My mother wouldn't ... You're lying! I've warned you!'

A vein was pulsing in his temple, like a worm wriggling away under his skin. He yanked his spectacles off, threw them onto the floor and stamped on them. Niven knew he'd brought him right to the edge but pressed on.

'Men are dead because of your mistaken belief. They weren't good men, far from it, but you killed them for the wrong reason. Now you're going to do the same again.'

He pointed at Brannigan. 'He did time for attacking your father. Justice was served. You've no right to play God.'

Perspiration dripped from Niven's brow as the gun swung to and fro between him and the convict. He was sure Thompson was trying to decide whom he should punish first, he thought his time had come.

'I tried to help you and your girlfriend,' Thompson whined, 'and you reward me by insulting my intelligence, besmirching the memory of my father.'

Niven glanced at Brannigan. Unless there was a miracle, any moment now they'd both be dead. It passed through his mind how strange it was he should come face to face with the man who'd helped to bring him into the world when they were both a mere finger twitch away from oblivion.

CHAPTER 40

The church door creaked on its hinges. Like a wanton child, a gust of wind swept in, searched out a pile of hymn sheets and chased them down the aisle. Behind the swirling sheets of paper, a figure appeared and started towards the three men at the altar.

Niven stared at the oncoming figure, sure his eyes must be deceiving him. The charlatan of a vicar was staring too, mouth open, as though he was seeing a ghost. The detective was completely thrown. There was no mistaking that blonde hair, those blue eyes. How could there be two Alan Thompsons?

'Alan!' the gunman gasped. 'You're not supposed to be here! I left—'

The teacher halted a few steps away, tears in his eyes.

'What are you doing, Brian?' he cried, his voice ridden with anguish. He held up the rumpled pages of a letter. 'Tell me you didn't do all this. Not you! Not my brother!'

Niven cursed himself for not seeing it. Now he understood. Those photographs on their mother's mantelpiece showed the Thompson brothers looked alike but hadn't done the similarity full justice, and obviously couldn't convey the similarity in their voices.

'You were staying at Mother's,' Brian muttered, 'leaving your mail for me to collect. Why did you—?'

'I decided to do the right thing, I moved back today,' the teacher snapped at him. 'My God, what have you done? How could you have killed those men!'

Brannigan snorted. 'He's mad, that's how – and my Darren's dead because he's mad!'

'Don't listen to him, Alan. I tried to explain in the letter. It was long past time I avenged our father. Those men I killed took him away from us.'

The teacher gave the sigh of a man near the end of his tether, shook his head sadly.

'He was a bent copper and a drug addict, Brian. The drugs turned his mind. That's why he hung himself.'

Puzzlement showed in PC's face. Then, his eyes narrowed suspiciously.

'You're making it all up to stop me, brother.'

Niven, after his initial confusion, thought it was time he spoke up.

'Think about it! We can't both be making it up, can we?'

'I heard a rumour about our father years ago,' the teacher continued, his voice melancholy. 'When I asked my mother about it she broke down, confirmed she had hidden the truth. Together, we decided to let you go on believing, thinking that was best.' He looked up at the cross with as pitiful an expression as Niven had ever seen. 'Our good intentions have backfired on us. We should have known the truth will always out.'

'Put the gun down and let it go,' Niven said. 'Don't make it worse than it already is.'

PC stared blankly at him, as though this was all too much for him and his mind was shutting down.

Alan Thompson saw the change and said softly, 'He's right, brother, give it up.'

PC didn't seem to hear. His face took on a haunted look of someone close to losing his sanity. After years of believing a myth, the truth about his father, the man who he'd been set on avenging, for whom he'd turned killer, was clearly too much for him to take. His body sagged forward and Alan Thompson chose that moment to step up closer, his hand extended to take the gun away from his brother.

Brannigan had waited for a chance. Seeing his son's killer was off guard, he lowered his head and rushed at him. His bulk hit PC full in the chest, knocking the breath out of him so that he staggered backwards, slipped on a step and went down. Following up his advantage, quick as a cat the criminal wrested the gun from his grip. An ominous silence ensued while, from the foot of the altar, where he lay as helpless as a sacrificial lamb, PC looked up at Brannigan and the gun with the weary indifference of a defeated, disillusioned man who knows he has nowhere left to go.

Two shots ripped into the silence. Blood spurted from PC's heart and a red stain spread over the white surplice. He tilted his head forward, touched the spot, stared at the blood on his fingers. Raising his eyes, he squeezed out words meant for Brannigan.

'You've done me a favour. Nothing left ...'

Brannigan backed away while Niven and the teacher rushed to the wounded man and cradled him between them as blood trickled from his mouth.

The detective stared up at the convict. That they shared the same blood filled him with horror. How could he shoot a man like that and stand there afterwards looking so unaffected? He'd already forgotten what he'd done and his eyes were everywhere, seeking an escape route. Niven couldn't help himself and spat out the words.

'I hope you rot in prison for this.'

As he spoke, he felt the dying man pull at his hand, with the last of his strength guide it underneath his surplice where it couldn't be seen towards something hard and metallic which was tucked into his waistband; Niven's fingers curled around a gun butt.

'Alan ... tell our mother ... I'm sorry.'

Those were Brian Thompson's last words. A moment later all the life went out of his eyes and his body flopped. Alan Thompson gave a cry of anguish and pulled his brother's body against his chest.

Brannigan was gazing down at them, his eyes cold and calculating. Niven didn't like that look. He tightened his grip on the gun butt. He didn't want to use the weapon, but, if it came to it, he was prepared to.

'Give up, man,' he snapped at the criminal. 'You've had your revenge – for what it's worth.'

Brannigan shook his head. His eyes were glassy, as though he was dreaming with his eyes open, part of him no longer with them. His next words seemed to be addressed to himself as much as them.

'You're the only witnesses. He killed both of you and I shot him before he had a chance to turn his gun on me – it was self defence.'

Realizing he had it in mind to kill them too, his stomach muscles taut with tension, Niven started to ease the gun out of the waistband.

'They'd work it out, man. Forensics would piece it all together in no time.'

'Worth the chance – what's to lose? 'Brannigan muttered. 'You're nothing to me.'

A cold draft of air wafted against Niven's cheek. He could hear the sound of his own breathing, was aware of Alan Thompson stirring beside him.

'He's going to do it!' the teacher called out as Brannigan started to lift the gun.

The warning was superfluous. A fraction before the criminal's weapon completed its upward arc, Niven drew the gun from under the surplice, took quick aim and fired. For the second time that morning the church resounded to the sound of gun shots, this time from two weapons in deadly competition.

Brannigan's shot went wildly astray. Niven's hit home. The criminal dropped his gun, hovered for what seemed an eternity, arms spread like wings, blood spurting from his chest. With a look of disbelief, he toppled, dying before he hit the floor. His lifeless eyes looked up at Niven, who was stunned by the magnitude of what he had done.

'You had to do it,' he heard Alan Thompson say. 'It was him or us.'

It was on the tip of his tongue to declare it was his father he'd shot, but he held back. It had been a secret in life, so why not in death? Noises came from the back of the church where armed policemen were rushing in and crouching behind the pews. A torrent of anger surged through Niven when he saw them, anger at their bad timing, anger at the whole world that it should have come to this.

'It's over!' he yelled. 'You're too late.'

With one last lingering look at the dead men and a whispered 'forgive me' to the figure hanging on the cross, he raised his hands, told the teacher to raise his. Together they started down the aisle, each aware he would never forget what had happened today, each with the weight of his own cross to bear.

CHAPTER 41

Bright light dazzled their eyes. Wind blown leaves danced around their feet, clung to their trouser bottoms like needy children. Someone threw blankets over their shoulders. Niven lifted his face up to the heavens where a patch of blue sky battled for space with grey clouds. He was alive! Lucky to have survived! He thanked God he'd at least see Gill again, be able to take care of her if she needed him.

The road bulged with police cars and ambulances, blue lights flashing maniacally. Beside them uniformed police stood in groups, heads swivelling towards the two, blanket-clad men emerging from the church. Niven hated being the object of attention and just wished it would all go away.

Johnson rushed towards them, flanked by officers and paramedics. Glad to see a face he recognized, Niven made an effort to pull himself together and spoke before his boss had a chance to.

'You'll find two dead men inside, sir, one of them Brian Thompson, the man we should have been after. The other is the criminal John Terrence Brannigan. Brannigan shot our man, then I had to shoot him in self-defence.' He inclined his head towards Alan Thompson. 'It's a long story but I was completely wrong about him. He saved the day.'

Johnson put a hand on his shoulder, gestured at the paramedics hovering nearby. 'You two look like you've been through hell. You're both going to hospital right now!'

'I'm OK!' Niven protested. 'Need to report! Straighten it out!'

'Not asking, son! Telling!'

Niven didn't argue. He felt drained. Maybe a nurse could stick a needle in him, replenish his energy.

'I'll get the full story after you've been checked out,' Johnson said.

Niven conjured the ghost of a smile. The brass would be wanting the facts from his boss yesterday, but Johnson was putting his welfare first. Not many in authority were as considerate.

The paramedics sprang into action, lifting them onto stretchers and then into an ambulance. It was a relief when the doors shut and hid them from all those curious eyes. Then, blue light flashing and siren wailing, the ambulance whisked them off.

Alan Thompson was lying directly opposite Niven. His face was drained of colour but he was still the spit of his brother, eerily so.

'I'm so sorry!' he said.

'What have you to be sorry for?' Niven asked. 'You saved the day. We had you down as the killer!. It's me who should be apologizing to you for that.'

'I mean, I'm sorry for what my brother's done. If only I'd told him the truth about our father.'

'You're not your brother's keeper.'

'Should have seen it coming.'

'How could you? How could anyone?'

Blue eyes bored into Niven's. Just for a second it was as though Brian Thompson had come to life again.

'Brian was dying – it was cancer – months left at most. He gave up his job – kept it all from me and Mother. The strain – I can't imagine. It was all in that letter.' Alan shook his head sadly. 'I can only think he must have gone mad.'

Niven heart reached out to this rather gentle schoolteacher. He doubted anything he could say would do much to alleviate his pain, but he gave it a try.

'For what it's worth, I think you're right about his mental state. You should let it rest at that because he's at peace and you need to be, for your mother's sake and your own.'

The teacher made an effort to pull himself together. A silence followed, neither man speaking because each was trying to reconcile the past with the present and finding it difficult.

Out of the blue, Alan said, 'He was one of you, you know, like Father was.'

Niven had no idea what that he meant.

'One of us?'

'Not exactly one of you, I suppose, but a special constable.'

Niven had blanked the man out of his mind because he'd felt so much resentment towards him, but now he recalled vividly the special who reported him for his treatment of Jack Cannon. He was nearly sure that special must have been Brian Thompson. He'd probably seen him with Gill. That red hair made her memorable. Maybe it had saved her life.

'You know, I've a hunch your brother saved my girlfriend's life,' he told the teacher, explained what he thought had happened at the warehouse.

'That's a little bit more like the brother I knew. At least he did some good amongst the mayhem he caused.'

'He must have recognized Gill was an innocent in trouble and helped her.'

Alan nodded. 'There's that, then.'

Back at headquarters, DI Johnson walked into his office and shut the door leaving the rest of the crew to continue celebrating the end of a long, hard investigation. DCI Snaith was due to come and see him within the next ten minutes for a debrief but he wanted time alone to gather his thoughts. From the moment he'd seen Niven emerge from the church, his face white and drawn, he'd been concerned about him, so much so he'd had no hesitation in sending him straight to hospital.

That decision had come easily but the next one was causing

him concern. For five minutes he vacillated before finally deciding there might never be a better opportunity than this for the course of action he'd been contemplating. Hoping he was doing the right thing for all concerned, he picked up the phone, dialed, and waited until the familiar voice answered.

'I think your time has come,' he said, getting straight to the point. 'Today he had to shoot a man in the line of duty.'

'Is he OK?' an anxious voice asked.

'Physically unharmed but mentally – who can say? These things can have immediate effect, or can manifest themselves years after the incident.'

'Where is he now?'

'Hospital, but just to get checked out. I'm expecting him back here soon. He did well, by the way.'

'Sounds like the time is ripe.'

'I think so, but back off if you get a bad reaction.'

'Don't worry, Tom, I'll go gently about it, I promise.'

'I know you will.'

'Who did he shoot?'

'Well, it hardly seems plausible but the fellow's name was—'

Before he could elucidate further he heard footsteps in the corridor, the sharp rat-tat rhythm of a man always in a hurry to get somewhere fast, knew they were DCI Snaith's.

'My boss is coming,' he said. 'No time now. Got to get off. Good luck.'

'You're a top man, Tom Johnson,' his friend said. 'Won't forget.'

After an hour of being examined and fussed over, Niven and Alan Thompson were told their ordeal hadn't done them any damage and shown to a rest room where an ample supply of tea and sandwiches awaited them. A nurse told them to get stuck in because a car would arrive soon to transport them to police headquarters.

While they were waiting, Niven drank his tea and studied the schoolteacher. Alan Thompson had conducted himself with dignity, he thought. In the church, he'd done his best to dissuade his brother, kept calm, hadn't panicked the criminal into losing his head. Though he had a touch of eccentricity about him, he seemed a good man and Niven felt he wanted to make up for his earlier misjudgement.

'I'll be speaking up for you, Alan. If it's any consolation, the way you behaved today under pressure must act in your favour concerning that other business. I'm sure the court will be lenient.'

The teacher managed a sad smile.

'That's considerate of you, but I'm finished as a teacher anyway. When the press find out I'm Brian's brother they'll have a field day, drag everything up from the past, suck the vestigial bones until they're dry. Who'll want to employ me in any job?'

Niven didn't know what to tell him. It was true: life would be much harder for him. Hopefully, there was someone out there who would judge him for himself, not for a mistake made under great duress, nor for his family's sins. He couldn't continue to be unlucky, could he?

'Must have been hard for you when you found out about your father,' Niven mumbled, adding poignantly, 'I can imagine what that was like.'

'Yes, it was awful.' The teacher, his movement ponderous, poured himself more tea. 'It made me determined I'd never be like him.'

Like a deep sea diver contemplating unfathomable depths of mystery, he stared at the floor.

'My brother became a nurse because he wanted to help people at their most vulnerable. He cared, you see. Whatever he did had nothing to do with inheriting our father's weak character.'

'Yes, I'm sure you're right. Must have had some kind of breakdown as you suggested earlier. All that business about PC 49 I told you about would seem to indicate he was way off centre.'

Niven was gracious enough not to point out how, though not through the genetic route, the sins of the father had still descended upon the head of the son, had reverberated in Brian's life, helping in the end to unbalance him.

There was a long silence, then Niven said, 'Everything pointed to you, Alan. I was on my way to take you in for questioning.'

The teacher sighed. 'People have always confused us.'

The detective's eyes drifted idly to an abstract painting hanging on the wall over the teacher's head. He could make nothing of it.

'How easily we can deceive ourselves,' he said, with a regretful sigh. 'I'm really sorry for thinking it was you, Alan!'

CHAPTER 42

DI Johnson leaned back, pushed out his stomach, loosened his tie, eyed Niven with an avuncular warmth. They'd just finished a session with the DCI. The big chief had departed very satisfied, bathing in reflected glory. A weight had been lifted from all their shoulders. They could relax now – until the next time.

'Thank God it's over!' Johnson exclaimed. 'It was brilliant work, just brilliant on your part, linking our killer to an incident so far back in the past.'

Niven blushed, hoped his boss wouldn't notice his embarrassment. He wanted to come clean, tell him it was his personal interest in finding more about Brannigan that had driven him to delve deeper than he might have otherwise. But his shame over his unwanted bond with the criminal was a barrier that he couldn't overcome. What made it all worse was the backslapping and congratulations he'd had to endure on his way in. It had been like the time he'd captured Jack Cannon; he felt so undeserving.

'I had the wrong man, sir. Alan Thompson was innocent. I'd convinced myself it was him. How clever was that?'

Johnson wafted a hand dismissively.

'Right family, wrong brother. You made a reasonable presumption. I was convinced too, remember.' He hesitated, cocked an eyebrow. 'What beats me is how you managed to turn up at that church at the critical moment?'

Niven forced a smile, tried to joke his way out of it.

'Try divine intervention for size, sir. The real vicar and his wife were praying hard. Maybe it worked and I was the instrument.'

Johnson stared at him. 'Come on now, don't give me that.'

Obviously, the DI wasn't going to let him off the hook as easily as that.

'I just happened to be passing. It struck me the funeral would be an opportunity for the killer to have a go at Brannigan. Pretty obvious really when you think about it.'

He didn't like stretching the truth, but what else could he do to satisfy his boss. Hopefully, it would suffice.

'So it was just lucky all round you were passing at that precise time?'

'Synchronicity, they call it, sir. It happens. Books are written about it.'

Johnson didn't look too convinced but he let it go.

'Synchronicity or not, you deserve the plaudits that'll be coming your way. Now get yourself home, son, get a good sleep. You OK to drive, by the way?'

Niven said he was fine. He was tired but he was determined to stop off at the hospital to visit Gill before he headed home, he didn't tell Johnson that, though.

'You'll be seeing a police psychologist tomorrow, son,' Johnson said. 'It's standard policy when you have to shoot someone in the line of duty.'

'If I have to, sir,' Niven answered, not happy about it as he rose and made for the door. Psychologists probed and he didn't want to keep lying about Brannigan. No doubt, if he confessed to patricide, they'd have a field day with him, try to turn his mind inside out. That was another reason to keep it buried.

Leaving headquarters was a massive relief. Answering questions had brought all the horror back; he'd felt he was reliving it. Killing a man was bad enough, but your own father?

In a church of all places? If the course of your life was pre-ordained, what kind of mind had thought that one up?

CHAPTER 43

Driving the well worn road to the hospital was therapeutic for Niven because it diverted his mind. As was usual these days, most of the parking spaces were occupied, but he found one at a distance from the hospital reception. He took a ticket from the machine, thinking he should have a season ticket he was here so often. Where did the exorbitant fees he paid end up? Someone must be making a profit, the hospital he hoped. But the money didn't matter when Gill was the reason for his visits? He prayed he'd find her improved so that an horrific day would end on a good note.

The first nurse he bumped into on the ward recognized him, smiled broadly giving him grounds for optimism. Surely she wouldn't be smiling at him like that unless there was good news.

He blurted out, 'How is she?'

'Much better. She's remembering more. The doctors are very pleased.' With a twinkle in her eye, the nurse added. 'In fact she looks better than you do. What happened – bad day or bad beer?'

He laughed, mainly with relief. If only she knew.

'She always looks better than me!'

'You said it, not me. Go in, see for yourself. I think you'll see an improvement, but please don't stay more than ten minutes.'

Gill was sitting up, a pile of pillows behind her back. Those grotesque tubes that crawled all over her like octopus tentacles, had disappeared. When she saw him enter, instead of that blank, fish-eyed look that pierced his heart, her eyes lit up with what he hoped was recognition. Almost afraid to blink in case this new Gill proved to be a mirage, he moved tentatively to the side of the bed.

'John!' she said, so softly he thought he might have misheard.

When she repeated his name, louder this time, he had no more doubt that she recognized him!

As he sat down, he reached for her hand, found there was warmth and strength in her fingers at last. Not for a moment did his eyes leave hers, which were as bright as he remembered them before the darkness descended, before she retreated to that place where he couldn't find her.

'Thank God,' he mumbled, holding back tears. 'Thank God!'

She reached out, touched his face, her touch like a balm after his horrific day.

'I can remember, John,' she said, a child-like joy in her eyes, as though she was discovering the world around her for the first time. 'I can remember everything up to the moment I entered the warehouse.' The childish joy left her, was replaced by a puzzled expression. 'After that it's a blank.'

It was on the tip of his tongue to tell her that blank was a blessing but thought it best to say nothing. If he told her it would distress her, might set her back. This moment felt like a miracle and he didn't want to spoil it.

'I thought I'd lost you,' he muttered, his voice husky.

Gill's eyes danced. 'Well, at least someone missed me. The nurses told me how devastated you were.'

He gazed at her, remembering the first time he'd ever seen her, how that face had seemed created just to please him, the kindness in her soul that reflected in her eyes and drew him in. What a fool he'd been to think he could walk away without visiting almost unbearable misery upon himself. What kind of aberration had he suffered?

'I do at least know why I went to that warehouse,' she said, suddenly, dropping her eyes, her tone serious. 'Do you know, John?'

'You did it for me, Gill, to find my father,' he answered, hoping that wouldn't stir up any bad memories for her.

Referring to Brannigan as father left a bad taste. His mind flashed back to his body lying at the altar. Then, he realized Gill was scrutinizing him and he pushed it all away.

'You know what happened in that warehouse, don't you, John? Please tell me.'

She was almost pleading, but he shook his head.

'Not now. Not until the docs say its OK. It might set you back. I don't want that.'

She looked disappointed, but seemed to accept he had her best interests at heart. Then, her face suddenly altered, became vague and distant as though a memory was stirring and she was trying to get to grips with it. He hoped he wouldn't have to fend off more awkward questions, not until she was much better. But in the end he needn't have worried because she left it alone and changed the subject.

'Your mother was here earlier,' she recalled. 'I know you've met her, John, and I think she's lovely.' She put her face in her hands and started to cry. 'I shouldn't have interfered in your business. I thought I was helping you, that you were depressed, but it wasn't my place to search for your parents.'

'None of that now,' he said sternly. 'You did it for my own good and I'm delighted I've met her. That was down to you, Gill. I probably would never have done it for myself.' He paused there a moment. 'Meeting her made a difference, you know. It was a kind of release for emotions I'd kept bottled up almost without knowing.'

He didn't, couldn't, tell her that as wonderful as meeting his mother had been, on the negative side it had led him into more turmoil than he could have imagined.

Gill brightened. 'I'm glad it has made a difference.'

'Yes! I know who I am now. As you say, my mother is a lovely woman. We got on like the proverbial house on fire.'

'And your father? You found him too? I remember now ... your mother mentioned—'

'Tell you about that later,' he said, cutting her off before they got too deep into that subject.

One good thing had emerged from all the trouble he'd been through. He knew he what he wanted in his personal life, what he needed. It probably wasn't the time or place to broach that subject but it just came straight out.

'I want to marry you, Gill, have a family. I mean – no pressure.' He looked down at his feet, mumbled. 'My timing stinks, doesn't it.'

When he looked up again, Gill was gazing at him, a half smile on her lips which he couldn't read.

'This isn't brought on by sympathy for the invalid, is it?' she said coyly.

'Not a bit. How could you think that?'

'Why then, John?'

She said it teasingly, but he knew she wanted an answer, that she deserved one. Where should he start? What should he leave out? For better or worse, he knew who he was now, and coming so close to death today had been a salutary reminder of the fleeting nature of this life, that time waited for no man. Dwelling too much on a past you couldn't change could destroy you. Brian Thompson was an example. But more than all that, the thought of losing Gill forever had been the real wake up call.

'I've been through Hell, Gill, and the upshot is I know you have to take a chance, that you can't build walls to protect yourself.'

'You changed your mind about children too?'

He nodded. 'They'll have all the security I can give them. After that, well, I have to hope life will be kind.'

Gill was quiet for a moment and he cursed himself for being premature. Why hadn't he waited until she was out of there?

'Ask me again later, John.'

'Sure, you need time. I understand – bad timing.'

Gill came back at him quickly, 'That's not it. I'm happy you asked but I can sense something has happened to you, so I'm giving you time to be certain you know what you want. If you're still sure, I'll marry you like a shot.'

'I'll be sure,' he said, brightening. 'It's the one thing I am sure of.'

He glanced at his watch, realized he'd stayed too long, told Gill the nurses would be telling him off if he didn't leave now. Kissing her goodnight, he walked out of the room, feeling more optimistic about his future than he had in a long time.

CHAPTER 44

'John! John Niven!'

He was passing the café on his way to the exit when the voice called out. He turned and saw his mother, as elegantly dressed as the day they'd met, waving at him from one of the tables. Sitting opposite her was a tall, well built man, around her age, dressed as smartly as she was. He started towards the café, conscious of the man's intense gaze as he approached them.

His mother rose, stepped forward to greet him, blocking his view of her companion. Slightly flustered, like a shy schoolgirl, she rose on tiptoe to kiss his cheek. Niven found that gesture strangely comforting, guessed, after what had happened in that church, affection was the medicine he needed.

'I've been meaning to ring you,' he said. 'But work's been ... horrific.'

He wondered whether he should tell her about Brannigan, decided the evils of the day were sufficient. It would keep for another occasion, but he wasn't relishing it.

She raised an eyebrow, slanted her head to one side in a half playful gesture, indicating to her son she wasn't entirely convinced his work had stopped him contacting her, that perhaps he was just making an excuse.

'No! Really!' he exclaimed, anxious to assure her he was being sincere. 'I have every intention ...' His voice drifted away, became lost in the clatter of plates and cutlery.

'I hope so,' she said. 'It means so much to me that you're in my life now.'

She shifted position so that he glimpsed her companion. He was studying Niven from head to foot, like a tailor measuring him for a suit. The intensity of his gaze disconcerted the detective a little. He wondered when his mother was going to introduce them but could see she was uncomfortable, fiddling nervously with the clasp of her handbag, not really sure what to say. When she did speak, it was with a hesitancy that seemed uncharacteristic.

'This is … an old friend,' A flush crept into her cheeks. 'He knows you're my son, John.'

The men nodded to each other. Niven had conducted enough interviews in his time to detect an atmosphere, words and thoughts held in check; he was pretty sure he could sense something of that nature here. His mother hadn't introduced her friend by name, which seemed strange, and neither his mother nor her friend seemed to want to take the initiative in the conversation.

Finally, when the silence dragged for rather too long, his mother spoke up, but again in that rather flustered manner.

'I've already been in to see Gill, but I'd like to pop back to the ward with some flowers for her. Would you mind keeping my friend company, John? I shouldn't be long.'

'Sure,' Niven said, wondering what she was leaving him with here. She seemed so anxious he didn't like to explain that he was very tired, wouldn't be very good company for anyone especially someone who, if first impressions were anything to go by, would hardly be the quintessential conversationalist.

'Gill told me you'd been in to see her. That was kind of you. We both appreciate it.'

His mother smiled, exchanged a meaningful look with her friend, then backed away from the table rather awkwardly, as though not sure she was doing the right thing leaving the two men alone. With a little wave that encompassed them both, she turned and went on her way.

The level of intensity in the man's gaze hadn't diminished. As he sat down, Niven felt like one of his own felons under intense scrutiny. He hoped they'd be able to find enough common ground to eat up the time while his mother was gone or it could get embarrassing. He didn't even know the man's name or, other than he was a friend, his relationship with his mother.

The buzz of conversation from the surrounding tables seemed amplified in contrast to their silence. His companion dropped his gaze, stirred his coffee over-conscientiously, raked his fingers through a thatch of grey hair. Niven held himself in check. Was there perhaps something bothering this man, something he needed to get off his chest? Perhaps he objected to his reunion with his mother. Whatever it was, he'd come out with it eventually.

Suddenly, he lifted his head, looked Niven straight in the eye. When he spoke, it was with a cultured voice, a touch authoritative too.

'Your mother left us alone on purpose because I need to tell you something that isn't easy for me to say nor, I imagine, will it be easy for you to hear.'

Niven locked eyes with him, wondering what this stranger could possibly have to say that merited such a dramatic build up? Whatever it was, the guy seemed deeply affected and it was clear his mother knew about it.

'You look a bit emotional to me,' the detective said, understating the case. 'I'm sure what you have to say doesn't warrant getting upset. Let me tell you I've had a difficult day, don't think anything you say can make it worse.'

Like a spy in a movie, the man scanned the surrounding tables, leaned forward conspiratorially.

'You can't even guess who I am?'

There was a pregnant pause, Niven struggling to remain patient because he was tired. He wished the fellow would just say whatever he had to say. After all, how bad could it be?

But when he made his announcement the words hit Niven with all the force of a flash flood springing out of nowhere.

'I have to tell you that I'm your father – Terrence Brannigan.'

Niven reeled backwards as though he'd been physically struck. Bile rose in his gullet, lingered at the back of his throat. He wondered if he could have misheard, but knew he hadn't. His first thought was that this character must surely have conned his mother into believing he was her first love, was trying it on with him for some nefarious reason he couldn't fathom. Well, he couldn't have chosen a worse day to test him.

'Of course you are!' he snarled. 'You're the daddy of them all, aren't you?'

The man's mouth dropped open. Whatever reaction he'd been prepared for, this wasn't one of them.

'Look,' he said, obviously shaken. 'This must be a terrific shock, but I assure you I am your father.'

Niven smiled coldly. 'Well, then, I'm sure I'd just love to call you Papa, but there's a problem – an insurmountable problem. What did you say your name was again, just so it's clear?'

'John Terrence Brannigan.'

Niven hit the table so hard with his fist that the crockery rattled and the cutlery jumped. The man opposite flinched. People at the neighbouring table stared but the detective didn't care.

'Well then, if that's who you're claiming to be, you're either a ghost who's got lost on the way to hell, or an impostor who, for reasons I can't begin to fathom, has managed to fool my mother.'

The man's face reddened. He looked bemused by the onslaught.

'Why would you think such things?' he gasped. 'I wouldn't fool your mother or you.'

'Because of a little incident that occurred today,' Niven snorted. 'A criminal was shot dead and I can vouch for that one hundred per cent because I was the detective who pulled the trigger.'

Niven paused, nose wrinkling in distaste as he looked the man opposite up and down as though he was something that had crept out of a sewer and a malodorous smell was wafting across the table.

'Life has its little tricks,' he continued. 'Earlier today it played one on me. Now it's your turn. The man I shot dead was – John Terrence Brannigan – my father.'

The man didn't evade Niven's accusing eyes, nor did he react with another made-up story, or anger, as the detective expected a charlatan exposed in a blatant lie might. But, then again, he had nowhere to go; except by claiming resurrection, how could he explain himself?

Yet, suddenly, his eyes became more alive, as though a revelation had come upon him. Niven guessed another lie was coming up!

'He was from Grove Hill, wasn't he, a scrap merchant of, shall we say ill-repute?'

'That would be gilding the lily,' Niven sneered, hiding his surprise that he knew so much. 'Now I suppose you're going to tell me there are two of you.'

The man shook his head emphatically.

'Hardly! However, my second cousin bore the same name as I do. It was passed down from a great-grandfather and long after two branches of the family had drifted apart.' He sighed. 'There were occasions when sharing that name caused problems but soon after you were born my family left the area and I know little about my cousin except he was a member of the criminal fraternity, a nasty character. My bet is that, by some quirk, it was him.'

Niven hadn't expected that but he was still sceptical. Improvisation, the ability to think on your feet, was an essential part of a con-man's repertoire. He studied the man's features closely, thought he could see a slight resemblance to himself. Or was that just his brain playing tricks?

'John, do you think that, even after all these years, I'd have changed to such a degree that your mother wouldn't recognize me? Do you think she'd have seen anything in a toe-rag like my cousin, a woman like her?'

Niven could see the logic, but he was still wary. Nothing in his life recently had been as it first appeared. Alan Thompson and his brother were examples. He wanted to believe this man, but was confused. Seeing his quandary, the man produced his wallet, extracted a photograph and laid it on the table.

'Take a look, John. That's a photograph of your mother and myself when we were teenagers.'

Niven leaned forward, studied it closely. The girl was very young, but he could tell it was his mother. The youth with one arm draped around her shoulders had the same features as the man opposite, was manifestly the same person.

'I can see it,' he mumbled, his mind in a whirl, aware his real father was watching him with a mixture of gentle understanding and a certain sadness in his eyes that would have been hard to manufacture. He put out his hand and his father clasped it eagerly. Embarrassed by his earlier reaction, he stumbled over his words.

'This has been the strangest day of my life and I'm not myself. Otherwise I wouldn't have—'

'You killed a man,' his father interrupted. 'How could you be yourself? No need for you to be sorry.'

The warm sincerity in his manner lifted Niven's spirits.

'I really am happy to meet you.'

With his mother, there'd been instant empathy. This wasn't the same. How could it be after that start? Yet, now that they'd cleared the doubts away, he did feel comfortable and there was a certain affinity there.

'I'm sorry for the way I abandoned you,' his father said, lowering his head. 'I was young, didn't fight hard enough for you or for your mother and the attitude of both families didn't help.' He sighed, brought his head back up. 'But they're just excuses, aren't they? I learned to live my guilt but believe me you've always been in my mind.'

Niven could tell by his manner he was sincere in his contrition and patted him on the hand.

'I was fine, you know. The couple who adopted me were the best. I did wonder occasionally but it didn't effect me until lately, after they'd both died. I felt like an orphan then.'

His father fidgeted with his teaspoon. 'Look, this may sound trite to you but I'd like to get to know you. It's far too late to be your father, but I'd like to be some part of your life. Mary feels the same, doesn't she?'

'No harm in getting to know each other,' Niven responded. 'There are things I'm curious about. How my mother tracked you down for instance?'

'Strangely enough I made contact with her earlier today. Quite a coincidence, almost as though it was meant to be.'

'What about your wife? I imagine it must have been difficult. Sometimes it's best to let sleeping dogs lie.'

'I'm a widower, John, but I told my wife you existed even before we married. I have a son, your half-brother. He's a few years younger than you, of course, but a good lad. I want you to meet him.'

'I'd like that.'

Niven was quite touched that both he and his mother wished to introduce their children to him. These last few minutes had an air of unreality about them. It was hard to believe what was happening, especially the timing of it all after the day he'd had.... The sight of his mother weaving her way through the tables was real enough, though, and he pulled out a chair for her.

She sat down, looking anxious, but his father was quick to reassure her everything was fine between them.

'Don't worry, Mary, John knows the truth. There was a slight misunderstanding which we soon cleared up and not worth going into. John has been very gracious, actually, and, I can only hope, forgiving.'

Niven shrugged his shoulders. 'Of course,' he said. 'Life's too short – and it ain't perfect.'

The tension vanished from his mother's face and the conversation started to flow. Niven was tired but happy and as curious about their lives as they evidently were about his. He drank two cups of coffee, the caffeine rush combating his tiredness.

Finally, his fatigue caught up with him and his mother noticed how hard he was fighting it. Unaware of the real cause, she suggested they were talking him to death and that he should go home to bed, that there'd be other opportunities to talk.

They walked out of the hospital, exchanging addresses and telephone numbers, promising to keep in touch and meet again, sooner rather than later. Niven watched his birth parents walk across the car park together and wondered whether there was spark left between them now. Probably not, he thought, given the passage of time. But you never knew. Life certainly had its surprises and he'd had more than his fair share.

As he drove home, he looked up at the stars over Teesside, thought about the two people who'd adopted him. In his heart, they'd always be his parents and he felt their absence every day. It was humbling to think what a leap of faith they'd taken when they'd adopted him. He owed them so much, not least for the example they'd set him in how to live his life. If they were out there somewhere and able to watch him, he knew they'd be pleased he'd found his other family.

CHAPTER 45

Niven glanced at Gill sitting beside him and said a small prayer of thanks. They were dining at Ivy Hotel near the village of Sedgefield on the outskirts of Teesside, the occasion was a double celebration, a gathering together of the members of his newly found family and the announcement of his wedding date to Gill. His mother and father were present for the meal, plus his half-sister and half-brother with their families.

Three months after leaving hospital Gill was as good as new. Her red locks were long and lustrous now, an outward manifestation of the fire that thankfully still burned just as bright within her in spite of her ordeal. Niven couldn't have been happier. He liked his new family, the warmth they displayed towards him the way they managed their children, his nephews and nieces, was firm, but loving. He thought it was a pity all children hadn't that privilege.

While everyone was chattering, he excused himself, headed to the men's room, but by-passed it for the front door, stood there looking out over the lake and woodland that formed the grounds of the hotel. It hadn't been by chance he'd chosen Ivy Hall. This was where his other mother and father had held their silver wedding and this moment of lone reflection was his way of including them in his day.

After a few moments of remembering and paying respect, he was conscious of a presence behind him. He turned to find his birth father gazing past him at the trees which encircled the lake like silent, watchful guardians.

'You owe them everything, don't you John?' he said. 'Guess right now you're wishing they could be here today.'

Niven was surprised he'd read his mind, took a moment to gather his composure.

'It seems strange that one of the last things he told me was not to look for you, to let sleeping dogs lie,' he said wistfully, then, staring deep into his father's eyes added, 'He was always wise, but this time I think he got it wrong.'

'Thought you had more faith in him than that, John. He had his reasons.'

Niven frowned. The remark sounded more like a pronouncement of fact, even a mild reprimand, rather than speculation, but before he could query it his father gave a resigned sigh and spoke again.

'There are things I have to tell you, John. Things you might not like to hear but which need saying. It's only fair you know about them and I've been working up to it for a while.'

More than a little bemused, Niven hesitated, then said, 'I think I'm virtually immune to surprises these days.'

His father looked him in the eye.

'He contacted me, John. Soon as he knew he was going to die he made the effort to find me, told me when he was gone you'd have nobody, asked me to watch over you.'

Niven could hardly believe what he was hearing. He swallowed hard. This was a surprise he wasn't immune to, one he could never have foreseen.

'You are – talking about my father – Will Niven.'

'Yes, of course! He said when he was gone I could decide the best moment to introduce myself. That would explain his let sleeping dogs lie, and I suppose if you'd searched me out it would have tilted the balance the wrong way, forced me into something he wanted me to do willingly.'

Suffused with emotion, Niven put his head in his hands. He was astounded that, one step from his grave, the old man had taken the trouble.

'There's something else,' his father continued, hesitantly. 'It was no coincidence I went to your mother that particular day. I'd already found out where she lived. Soon as I knew what happened to you in the church I went straight to her and was surprised to learn you two had already met. We gambled you'd turn up at the hospital.'

Niven frowned. 'The same day? You knew about my involvement in the shooting that same day? How could you possibly?'

His father fiddled with his jacket buttons, didn't seem to know where to put his hands. Finally, when he'd imprisoned them in his trouser pockets, he gave a sigh and explained himself.

'I've snooped on you a bit, John. You won't like that, I'm sure, but my intentions were well meaning.'

'Snooped!'

'Wrong word, maybe. You see, in another life I was a copper. Your DI Johnson and I were trainees together and good friends in our youth. When Will Niven told me you were a working for Johnson the three of us came to a little arrangement.'

Niven was mystified. 'A little arrangement? What kind of arrangement?'

His father hesitated, seemed to have to go deep within himself before he could elaborate. When he spoke, he kept watching his son as though afraid of his reaction, that his words might fracture the relationship they were still building.

'With his own proviso that no way would he ever treat you differently from your colleagues, Johnson would keep me informed about your welfare and I'd introduce myself if ever you needed someone to be there for you, as they say. All a bit clumsy, I suppose, but better than barging in straight after Will's death. On reflection, it wasn't the best plan, but we all agreed I'd be there in a crisis.' He blushed. 'I even made a phone call to Gill when I heard about the Cannon business.'

Niven's first reaction was anger. He felt like a schoolboy who needed looking after. Even his boss had been in on it. But his initial spark of temper died quickly. Knowing who he was, coupled with all he had come through, had given him a calmer approach to his life over the last months. Seeing the anxiety plainly written on his father's face, he couldn't hold it against him. End of the day, he'd been doing what he thought best.

'Sorry if I've caused you any great offence,' his father muttered, 'I wouldn't—'

'No offence,' Niven cut in. 'In fact, I guess I have to consider myself lucky. The old man gave you a chance to turn your back and you haven't. If you passed his test that has to be good enough for me.'

His father's facial muscles relaxed. Grinning his relief, he put his hand around Niven's shoulders.

'Thank God for that,' he said. 'Now let's go join your family.'

As they strolled back to the restaurant, Niven came face to face with Alan Thompson. The teacher was smartly dressed and looked nothing like the man whose surfeit of trouble had brought him close to a breakdown.

'So you decided to accept my invitation after all?' Niven said as they shook hands. 'Better late than never.'

Alan jerked a thumb over his shoulder.

'Just popped in with a present for you and Gill. I've left it at reception.

Niven was touched. 'That was kind of you.'

'Well, you did your best for me. Maybe if you hadn't I'd have had more than a suspended sentence.'

'This is ... my father,' Niven said.

Those words still felt a little strange. He didn't introduce him by name because the name Brannigan would have stirred all those memories that Alan Thompson needed to bury.

The teacher nodded at Terry, eyed Niven. 'You're lucky to have a good father.' A dark shadow flitted across his face. 'Wish mine had been!'

His father looked a little embarrassed by the irony in that

statement and Niven felt for him. Poor Alan! He'd drawn a losing ticket in the paternal stakes and the repercussions had been horrendous.

They said their goodbyes, promising to keep in touch. Back at the table, he didn't have much time to settle because as soon as he took his seat he was called upon to make a speech, something he hadn't been prepared for. Speeches were never his forte, so it was not without a little trepidation that he climbed to his feet, hoping he could improvize something half-sensible.

'I'm a lucky man,' he said. 'For a little while I was lost. You people here today helped me find myself again – so I know who I am now.' He glanced down at Gill, 'and I am twice blessed because I'm going to marry the only woman for me.'

He sat down to a round of applause, hoping he'd said everything he should. When the applause died, his father, encouraged by his mother, climbed to his feet and rapped on the table calling for silence.

'John is too polite to say it,' he began, 'so I want to say it for him. You see, the reason John is with us today is that his adoptive parents, Will and Pat Niven, brought him up to be a decent human being. Will, in fact, made this gathering possible because he cared enough to make sure John would have his family around him when he was no longer here. So, on what is a joyful day for Mary and me, I'd like you all to raise a glass to Will and Pat Niven and the debt we can never repay.'

It was a gracious speech and Niven was touched. As glasses clinked and the room resounded to Will and Pat's names, he sensed the past merging with the present, something coming full circle exactly the way Will and Pat Niven would have wanted.